Designer Label
eleanor davies

Scripture
Union

By the sme author
In the Spotlight

For Mary

Copyright © Eleanor Davies 1998
First published 1998
Reprinted 2001

Scripture Union, 207-209 Queensway, Bletchley,
Milton Keynes, MK2 2EB, England.

ISBN 1 85999 212 9

British Library Cataloguing-in-Publication Data.
A catalogue record of this book is available from the British
Library.

Printed and bound in Great Britain by
Cox & Wyman Ltd, Reading, Berkshire.

1

Sat 12th Oct: Squirrel's 70th birthday party.
Problem is, I've got nothing to wear. Mum wants me to wear a dress, or at least a tidy skirt, as my three little cousins are bound to be all be dressed up. Only dress I've got is my old denim pinafore which is much too small and makes me look about ten. Why can't I wear jeans like Josh?

Suppose I might get away with it with the bib part rolled under the waistband. With a jumper over the top no one can tell, and I can pull it up to make it look a bit shorter. Must do something about my clothes.

Squirrel's party was quite an occasion, all the cousins and aunts and uncles were there. My mother was right about the cousins. They came in matching dresses in pale pink flowery material and pale pink ribbons in their hair. I wondered how long it would be before Joey, the eldest, who was nearly eight, went on strike and demanded a black lycra micro skirt. Josh, my eleven-year-old brother, got away with wearing his old jogging bottoms from Tesco's; obviously the rules were different for boys. I guessed Mum knew he'd escape into the garden to play football at the first opportunity and couldn't stand the thought of washing grass stains off good trousers. (Rather surprising, bearing in mind her usual obsession with hunting down things to wash.)

Squirrel seemed to enjoy her party. It was hard to believe she was really my grandmother; she never seemed to get tired. She's got lots of wrinkles like other people of her age, but somehow you never think of her as old. Her current craze is computer games – she is the only person I know who can beat Josh's score at Space Olympics. The family had all clubbed together to buy her a crystal vase for her birthday and she was very polite, but I suspect she would have preferred a Play Station. I don't think Mum and Dad had got over the shock of her last craze yet; I mean, how many people take up windsurfing in their late sixties? Passers-by on the sea front will never forget the amazing sight of the little grey-haired old lady, whooping with delight as she rode the waves, desperately trying to avoid ramming into the serious surf freaks in shiny black wetsuits who sped across her path.

'…Mother, don't you think at your age?…'
'…have you forgotten your bad back?…'
'…perhaps grow old gracefully?…'

The food at the party was really good. It was one of those occasions where everyone brings something in a Tupperware box and all the aunts are secretly trying to outdo each other in their culinary brilliance. There was no one I particularly wanted to talk to, so I decided to find a quiet corner and conduct a Scientific Quality Control test on the relative merits of Auntie Val's trifle,

4

Aunt Sue's pavlova and my own mum's chocolate mousse. Actually the mousse was partly Josh's work, and I was a bit worried about the hygiene aspect, having seen the chocolatey state of his face during its creation.

'Charlotte dear!'

Auntie Val (mother of the three pale pink flowery dresses), bearing a portion of fresh fruit salad. She's the only person who always calls me Charlotte instead of Charlie. I took a large mouthful of meringue and waited for the usual three conversation openers: (a) my immense rate of growth, (b) my GCSE subjects and (c) my life's ambitions.

'Charlotte dear, how pretty you look! Where did you get that lovely skirt? I won't say how tall you've got – I know how boring that is for you young things. So, how's school? Have you started your GCSEs yet? What are you going to do when you leave?'

Unfortunately I was unable to speak, as a particularly gooey piece of Aunt Sue's meringue (five out of ten) had stuck itself to my brace. Before I could separate my jaws sufficiently to make a reply, Auntie Val let out an agonised howl at the sight of Josh through the French window, rugby tackling the smallest pale pink dress in a flowerbed. Without waiting to hear the finer details of my planned career as a supermodel, my aunt set off at high speed to rescue her precious darling from the nasty dirty boy, while I added her portion of fruit salad to the Quality Control test. Pity to waste it, after all.

I caught Squirrel's eye across the room and she winked.

I found myself wishing I had an *older* cousin, preferably a boy.

Sun 13th Oct.
Church in the morning. Junior Pilgrims as usual. For some
reason, felt really depressed.

    I seem to be the oldest everywhere I go. I'm the oldest
in our family, the oldest amongst the cousins and the oldest person at JPs. It's horrifying to think that Josh has
nearly reached the age when he could belong too, along
with all his repellent little friends. It's another three
months before I'll be old enough to go up to Senior
Pilgrims. I don't know what I'd do without Becky and Kate;
in fact, I might try to get out of going if it wasn't for the
fact that I couldn't desert them. Of course, Becky'll have to
go to church for ever, being the vicar's daughter.

Junior Pilgrims always takes place in St Matthew's
church hall while the adults are in the morning service.
Actually the meeting was quite exciting this particular
Sunday as we had a guest speaker: an amazing girl who
had come all the way from London to tell us about her
dramatic conversion to Christianity. She was very beautiful and sort of shiny, (fantastic moon-shaped earrings)
and had a name which I didn't quite catch but sounded
something like Samantha Sparkle. Apparently she'd had
a really shady past as a dancer in a Soho night-club and
had been addicted to drink and drugs, turning to a life
of crime to support her habit. She began to describe it
all in great detail; but unfortunately Elaine, our JP leader,
who was inclined to take her leadership responsibilities
very seriously, stopped her in mid-flow and said, 'Gosh,
Samantha, how fascinating, but we're very short of time,
so could you move on now to the bit where your life
changed?' This was very disappointing; we could have
listened for hours to stories of her sordid past. Anyway,
it seemed that eventually a passing evangelist had come

into the nightclub and told her about Jesus, and wham! her whole life was revolutionised. The effect her conversion had on her was so dramatic that now she devoted her whole life to going round clubs in London and telling her story to anyone who was prepared to listen, in the hope that they too could find God.

I discussed what she'd said afterwards with Becky and Kate over polystyrene cups of lukewarm tea in the church hall.

'Wasn't she *awesome*?' breathed Becky, who tended to get very enthused about that sort of thing.

I agreed that she had been truly inspirational and added, 'The trouble with people like her is that she makes your own life seem so boring. I mean, what sins have you committed this week? Mine have been not tidying up my bedroom, and kicking Josh when he switched over to Ceefax for the football results while I was trying to watch 'Home and Away'. Oh, and I swore when I dropped my French dictionary on my toe – but it wasn't a very *bad* swear word. Somehow it all seems rather trivial compared to a stirring story like hers.'

'I know what you mean. It must be so exciting to have your life change so dramatically,' sighed Becky.

'The thing is,' I went on, 'perhaps if I had a really juicy past, the whole God thing would seem a bit more thrilling. But growing up in a home with parents who never miss an opportunity to drag me off to church, I can't really remember a time when I haven't believed in God. It all seems to make sense, it's the right thing to do, it's just that sometimes it all seems so dull.'

'But surely we're supposed to be the lucky ones, having a stable home and everything?' said Kate, who always looked at things sensibly.

'Well, yes, I suppose so. But I wouldn't mind *trying* a

day or two of serious sin – just to see what I'm missing.'

Kate looked rather shocked at this, which was satisfying. She was quite easily shocked.

I was thinking about this conversation as I walked home from the bus stop after school a couple of days later, and decided to call in on Squirrel on my way. This was partly to get her views on the subject, and partly because double chemistry followed by maths had made me extra hungry, and I knew there was usually something nice to eat in her larder. She was making blackberry and apple jam, and her kitchen was all steamy, but, as always, she was delighted to see me. Her new vase stood on the sink, full of bright yellow chrysanthemums.

'You've arrived just at the right moment,' she told me, 'I was just wondering how I was going to reach my jam labels. They're in a box in that high cupboard over there. Be an angel, would you?'

I climbed up on a stool and opened the cupboard. Immediately, an avalanche of margarine tubs, egg boxes, empty loo rolls and plastic bags cascaded onto the floor: in fact it seemed like the entire props cupboard of the Blue Peter studio. This, of course, is how Squirrel acquired her name; she is always ferreting things away in case they come in handy later. Her bedroom drawers are full of intriguing old hats and scarves, and an amazing collection of unwearable and quite worthless jewellery. Mum once embarked on one of her clearing out missions and found no less than thirteen pairs of glasses, all with out-of-date prescriptions, lurking in various drawers. She also found six bottles of laxative in varying stages of emptiness, skulking at the back of the medicine cupboard. A moving moment.

'Squirrel,' I said, in between writing labels to stick on

8

the jars, 'Don't you ever feel that you would have had more fun if you'd been a bit less upright?' I realised as soon as I'd said this that it was a stupid question, no-one got more fun out of life than Squirrel.

However, she considered the idea for a moment. 'I don't think so,' she said at last. 'Although sometimes other people's lives look more attractive, you don't know what's going on *inside*. But you have to decide which things are important. There are some things like wearing rings in your eyebrows or dyeing your hair green that might not be very acceptable at your church, but actually they don't really matter one way or the other. And there are other things like being kind and honest and reliable that actually matter very much indeed, and your life certainly won't be more fun if you ditch those. You have to think about each thing that life throws at you and decide whether it is something that really matters. If it is, then you won't be happy if you compromise what you believe.'

'So why is it that people who don't go to church often seem so much more exciting than those that do? People like Sabrina, for instance.' Sabrina was my best friend at school.

'Hum. That's a difficult one. Perhaps some of the churchgoers have forgotten that they are meant to enjoy God's world. If you're alert, God can teach you through everyone and everything. Only, you have to work out what is from him and what isn't. Do you want to take some of this jam home?'

Tues 15th Oct.
Is it possible to be a Christian and still have fun?
Sabrina seems to have a brilliant life most of the time.
Admittedly she went through a bad time last year when

9

her parents got divorced, but she still sees loads of both of them. In fact they both seem so keen to make sure she is happy that they never stop thinking of ways to entertain her. She's allowed a lot more freedom than me and gets to go on extra holidays with her dad, and what's more, she doesn't have an idiot younger brother at home to cramp her style. Sometimes can't help noticing how much more fun she is to be with than Becky and Kate. Lucky that they're at a different school, not Tatbury High, don't think they'd mix very well with Sabrina. It's not that Sabrina's actually bad, just that her ideas for livening up a Saturday afternoon aren't necessarily the sort of thing I'd always want to explain in great detail to Mum. But she's one of the kindest people I know.

I was slightly late for school the next day but Mr Larkin didn't notice because he was too busy telling Sabrina off for coming into school with a nose stud.

'This isn't the first time I've had to speak to you about this sort of thing, is it, Sabrina?' he was saying in a doleful voice, not so much cross as resigned.

'No, Mr Larkin. Sorry, Mr Larkin,' said Sabrina patiently.

'Well, don't let me see it again. Or there will be serious trouble.'

Sabrina returned to her seat next to me and muttered, 'Can't think what all the fuss is about. The new art teacher has a nose stud and no one complains about *her*. But if I say that to Mr Larkin I'll be told off for being cheeky. You can't win.'

It was true, you couldn't. Personally, I thought the stud looked very good.

'Anyway,' she went on, 'what shall we do on Saturday? I've got quite a good idea if you can't think of anything.'

'Oh no, not another of your ideas. What is it this time?'

'I thought I might get a tattoo. There's a place just off Market Square where you can get them done. Don't look so horrified, Charlie, they're all the rage.'

'I'm not looking horrified,' I said, lying, 'I think it's a brilliant idea. I'll definitely come with you. But not a great big one like you see on men digging the road: something small and tasteful like a butterfly or a flower.'

'Yes,' said Sabrina, 'exactly what I had in mind.'

However, when we went into town that Saturday it didn't take us long to discover that you had to be eighteen to get a tattoo; and although Sabrina might almost have passed for eighteen in a dim light, it would have been a waste of time for me even to try. Instead we got temporary tattoos – they looked just like the real thing, but were done in a dye that would wear off after a week or so. Sabrina felt deeply humiliated at having to resort to this, she reckoned they were not much better than kids' transfers, but secretly I was very relieved. I'm not sure how I would have explained it to Mum. Mine was a rosebud, Sabrina's was a peacock with its tail all spread out.

I showed my new tattoo to Kate in the Resources Cupboard at church the next day. Excellent reaction, she nearly fainted with horror.

'Charlie, what can you be thinking of! It'll never come off – you're stuck with it for life!'

I gave a nonchalant shrug of the shoulders. 'So?' It hardly seemed worth mentioning that my decoration was temporary, so I didn't. Was it admiration I saw in her face, or uneasiness? Or both?

Meanwhile Mum was busy inviting Becky's Mum round for a cup of tea next Saturday afternoon.

'Oh no, nothing special,' I heard her say, 'just take us as you find us... Oh and do bring Becky too, Charlie would be so pleased.'

Why do parents do things like that? Had she forgotten I always spend Saturday afternoon with Sabrina? When we got home I crossly reminded her that I wasn't free on Saturday afternoons, but she didn't seem at all bothered.

'Never mind,' she said. 'You can have them both round together. It would be nice for them both to meet someone from another school. You never know, perhaps Sabrina will like Becky so much she'll start coming to Junior Pilgrims.'

Sometimes I wondered if Mum understood *anything*.

I came home from school a couple of days later to be greeted by the sight of a strange, round, leathery brown object sitting on the kitchen table. No sign of Mum. Josh was sitting on the living-room floor watching television amongst the contents of his school bag, his mouth full of biscuit.

'Josh, what's that thing in the kitchen? And where's Mum?'

'Jus' popped round to Squirrel's. Can't remember why. Recipe or something. It's bread, I think.'

I examined the strange brown object to see if he was telling the truth and decided he was fibbing. Perhaps it was a meteorite from outer space which had sailed through the window when she was shaking her duster out.

Wed 23rd Oct.
Strange brown object mysteriously disappeared. Thought I saw it under a pile of tea leaves in the bin but couldn't be sure. Mum cleaned the fridge today.

12

Thurs 24th Oct.
Another strange brown object in kitchen, this time with lumpy knobbly bits on it. I suppose it could be bread. Mother in diabolical mood, insisted on us tidying every room in the house. Bathroom has weird disinfectant smell.

Fri 25th Oct.
Mum had third attempt at what is now clearly bread. Dad told her not to give up her day job.

This time it came out oblong with a deep crater in the middle, but Dad, who for some reason couldn't stop laughing, pointed out that if you stood it upside-down you couldn't see the crater. This seemed to cheer Mum up very slightly and she wrapped it carefully in a polythene bag and put it in the bread bin. When Josh asked if he could have a slice with his spaghetti bolognese, she got very irritable and snapped, 'Don't be so silly, Josh, it's not for *eating*!'

I woke the next day to the sound of the Hoover outside my room. Wrapping myself in a duvet, I wandered downstairs to join Josh, who was watching obscure popstars taking phone calls about their favourite colours, interspersed with cartoons of teenage superheroes rushing about saving the environment from the sinister effects of oil pollution.

'Ssh,' he said automatically, without looking up. I threw myself on the sofa, reflecting that in my day the cartoon heroes had to fight much more fearsome adversaries: people like Wolf Fang, Prince of Doom, and Deadly Laser Man, a cheery fellow who could demolish Los Angeles with nothing more than a long, hard look.

There was a nice smell of baking cakes. On the coffee table someone had left a pile of books with titles like

Happy Families — how to be a Model Mother and *Serene Parenting and how to achieve it*. Strange.

A bloodcurdling scream rang out from the kitchen. Rushing through, I found Mum wringing her hands and the kitchen awash with pale grey water. The washing machine had flooded.

'Just when I wanted everything to be so nice!' she wailed. 'I knew it was making a peculiar noise on Monday. Why on earth didn't I get the engineer out then?' Recognising a Crisis when I saw one, I abandoned my duvet and went to fetch a bucket and mop, wondering why everything had got to be so special today. Surely not just because Becky and her mum were calling in for a cup of tea? Into my mind drifted a conversation I'd had with Mum about what a wonderful family the Soames were, and how the children were always so well-behaved, and how their mum made all their clothes, and what a wonderful cook she was and made her own bread, and... Ah. Could there be a link here?

2

Sabrina appeared soon after lunch looking absolutely stunning in a minute black skirt and a tight low cut white T-shirt. She'd still got the remains of her suntan from the summer and she was so dark she looked almost Spanish. I could see my mother eyeing the plunging neckline with a disapproving stare, but she said nothing.

'Do you want to come upstairs to my room?' I said, leading the way up. 'I've got that CD I've been dying to play you.' We made ourselves comfortable on the floor in my bedroom and settled down to a game of cards.

There was a thump on the door. 'Can I play?' yelled Josh from outside.

'No! Go away!' I shouted back. He was hopeless at cards; it was a waste of time letting him join in. He sat on the floor with his Gameboy in the passage outside the room and sulked.

At half past three the doorbell rang and Becky and her mum arrived. From the top of the stairs I could hear my mother moving into Sparkling Hostess Mode.

'Ann, dear! And Becky! Do come in. Becky, you'll find Charlie and Sabrina upstairs in Charlie's room; just follow the music. Now, Ann, do come through to the living-room, I'm so glad you found time to pop in. I'll put the kettle on, and with any luck I may have a bit of old cake somewhere in a tin out in the kitchen.' I could hear her bustling through to the kitchen to collect the new fruit cake and fresh shortbread that were still cooling on the rack. I wondered where Dad was. I had a vague recollection he had taken himself off to the garden centre for the afternoon, and who could blame him?

Becky materialised at the bedroom door in an identical pair of jeans to mine and a long blue shirt. She looked about five years younger than Sabrina even though there were only about two months between them. I introduced them and they smiled politely at each other. Long silence.

'Sabrina and I were just playing cards,' I said brightly. 'Do you want to play?'

'OK. As long as it's something I know.'

Two noisy rounds of Racing Demon later the awkwardness had completely dissolved, and Sabrina and Becky were chatting away happily when Mum called us down for a cup of tea. She was just filling the pot as we came into the kitchen, and Becky's mum Ann was standing chatting to her.

'Oh no, we hardly ever watch *Neighbours*,' I heard my mum saying, 'we'd all much rather read a good book.' This was rich, considering she'd made me video Tuesday's episode when she was working late, in order not to miss the bit when the Coffee Shop was wrecked by vandals.

Ann had caught sight of the upturned loaf casually lying on the bread board on the kitchen table. 'I didn't know you made your own bread, Helen,' she said in surprise.

'Didn't you?' said Mum airily. 'Well, it's so much nicer, isn't it?' She quickly steered Ann back towards the living-room before she could get a closer look at the offending item, and we three girls pounced on the remaining cake and took it upstairs to devour.

By the time that Ann was ready to leave, Sabrina and Becky seemed like old friends. It was in the middle of an intense discussion about shades of eyeshadow that Becky seemed to be suddenly struck by an idea.

'You should come to our church on a Sunday morning,' she said. 'It'd be really good fun if you came with Charlie.'

Sabrina looked surprised. 'What, singing hymns and praying and all that sort of thing? I don't think so. Not my style at all.'

I had a mental vision of the sophisticated Sabrina in her tiny skirts singing choruses amongst the likes of Gavin Sykes and Robbie Jones in their dreadful yellow football shirts. I imagined her listening to one of Elaine's talks on Witnessing at School and pictured her the following Monday morning politely saying she didn't think she'd come again, and perhaps as we had a slightly different view of life from each other maybe we wouldn't sit together quite so much.

I shuddered deeply.

'Oh Becky, I'm sure Sabrina's far too busy – anyway how would she get there? And…'

'It's all right, Charlie,' said Sabrina, 'I always spend Sunday with my dad anyway. So it's out of the question.'

I suppose, all things considered, the afternoon could have been worse.

Mon 28th Oct: *Half-term week.*
Mum still trying to be the perfect parent. Suspect she feels the teeniest bit guilty about the act she put on for Ann Soames and is trying to ease her conscience by making her new image rather more permanent. Wouldn't mind if it didn't affect me so much. Spent the first day of precious half-term week having a mega clear-out of my bedroom. I need hardly say, this was not my idea. Found all sorts of interesting things stuffed down the back of my desk, including the school copy of 'Twelfth Night' which I was supposed to hand in at the end of last term.

Josh wasn't very impressed with the New Improved Mother either, particularly when she started tightening up on his bedtime. He usually gets away with being sent upstairs and then surreptitiously reading football magazines in bed, until someone notices his light is still on and yells at him. Mum had obviously decided to put a stop to all that. She started removing the whole pile of magazines every night and turning his light out at nine o'clock sharp. I could hear him through the wall when I went up, lying in bed and muttering to himself.

She even started trying to reform Dad, making him walk to work instead of driving, as apparently he needed more exercise. It absolutely poured with rain on Tuesday, but as Mum had taken half-term week off, she didn't seem to notice the weather. Poor Dad, he had to change all his clothes when he got home.

'David Soames walks everywhere,' she said, when he complained.

'David Soames is the vicar. He only has to go round the parish. It takes me over half an hour to walk to work. Look, I appreciate your concern for my health, but I'm afraid in this case the threat of pneumonia is greater than the threat of a heart attack. Sorry.'

Mum opened her mouth and then closed it. She knew better than to argue any more. Dad is usually a very gentle person, but he can be amazingly obstinate when the occasion requires it, and this was definitely one of those occasions.

'I shouldn't worry, Charlie,' he said when I moaned to him in a quiet moment, 'it won't last long. She obviously really admires Becky's mum and feels she's got to be just like her. But in the end we're all different and we can't try and be something we're not. She'll soon go back to being herself again. I bet you have friends you try to impress in just the same way.'

I thought about this. 'Well, yes, I suppose I do worry about what people at school think of me. Especially over clothes and things like that.' I remembered how I had felt at the thought of Sabrina coming to Junior Pilgrims and realised that I was fairly selective about which bits of me she was allowed to see. I supposed Mum was the same with Ann.

Thurs 31st Oct.
Dad was right. House is beginning to look untidy again. Spotted a sliced white loaf in the freezer. Things are looking up. Although interestingly, Mum has been reading one of those books she left lying around, and seems to be really enjoying it. And Dad walked to work again today without being told to; said he quite enjoyed the fresh air. Strange things, parents.

Sun 3rd Nov.
Junior Pilgrims. Doing Old Testament heroes at the moment; today we did Samson. Not one of my better Sundays.

Elaine asked Kate to read the story from Judges to us, and while she was reading I suddenly remembered a book I'd had when I was little. On the front was a picture of a banqueting hall full of unsuspecting Philistines, feasting on bunches of luscious purple grapes and golden goblets of wine. In the middle stood the ultimate party pooper: a wild black-haired Samson, blind eyes rolling scarily, poised between the two pillars which were about to get the mighty heave-ho. The memory of this gave me a bright idea.

'Why don't we act it, Elaine? It'd be really good. One of us could be Delilah and one could be Samson and the rest of us could be the Philistines.'

'Oh yes!' said Becky, the ever loyal friend. 'What a brilliant idea, Charlie! You could be Delilah. Couldn't she, Elaine?'

Elaine looked slightly nervous. 'We-ell, I suppose we *could* do some drama. I must say, I hadn't really planned...'

'Oh, please!' several voices came at once.

'There's really only two real characters,' said Elaine, uncertainly, 'and not much for the Philistines to do. Which of you would be Samson?'

Robbie Jones' hand shot up. He was wearing his goalkeeper's Away Strip today, with a multicoloured shirt that looked as if someone had been very ill over it. 'I'll be Samson!'

'There we are, then,' I said briskly, before Elaine could bring up any more objections.

The Philistines were already gathering together on one side of the hall and arguing about what weapons they should arm themselves with. I racked my brains to think of something to tie up the sleeping Samson with and eventually hit on the idea of borrowing some tea towels from the kitchen at the back of the hall. They were a bit small so I tied three together, hoping the Mothers' Union wouldn't miss them when they came out to make the coffee after the service.

Gavin Sykes, who had appointed himself as Chief Philistine, was carefully re-reading the passage through in his Bible. Having got the general gist of his part, he put the Bible down and strode purposefully towards me.

'So, Charlie, I mean, Delilah!' he declaimed in his most Shakespearean voice, 'it's up to you! Find out what it is that makes Samson so strong and we'll make it worth your while!'

He patted his side meaningfully, and the small change he had brought to contribute to the usual collection for missionary work rattled in his pocket.

'Right!' I said. Adopting my most appealing smile I turned to Samson, who was trying out various poses to demonstrate his immense muscles. 'Tell me, Samson, what is the secret of your great strength?'

Samson looked slightly nonplussed. 'I can't remember,' he muttered.

Kate, who was still holding her Bible, decided to take on the role of prompter.

'Seven new bowstrings!' she hissed in a stage whisper.

'Oh yes, that's right. Tie me up with seven new bow-strings and I''ll be as weak as everyone else.' He stood there, flexing his biceps, looking pleased with himself.

'Go to sleep, then, dear Samson,' I ordered, patting the floor next to me.

He lay down on the dusty hall floor, snoring loudly. I squatted beside him and tied his feet together very securely. There were no more tea towels to tie his arms.

'The Philistines are upon you, Samson,' I cooed in his ear.

He jumped to his feet, ready to throw off his bonds. Unfortunately I had tied them much too tightly, so he simply tripped and fell flat on his nose.

'That's not fair, Charlie!' he protested. 'I'm supposed to be able to break free!' He sat down and started picking at the towels, but the more he pulled, the tighter the knots became.

The Philistines were all starting to titter in the background. Elaine decided to intervene.

'Perhaps you could *pretend* you managed to break free,' she suggested. 'It will take ages if Charlie keeps tying you up and untying you, and everyone will be out of the service in a minute wanting their coffee. Why don't you skip the bits where Samson keeps telling lies to Delilah, and go on to the bit where he tells her the *real* secret of his strength.'

Robbie looked disgruntled. 'But I wanted to show my great strength!'

'Well, you can do that in a minute when you pull the house down,' I pointed out. 'Now, Samson, this is your last chance: what is the secret of your great strength?'

For a minute I thought he was going to go on strike, then he said grudgingly, 'It's in my hair.'

'Aha!' I exclaimed and started looking round for a suitable tool for cutting his hair off. However, Kate, who sometimes seems to have a sixth sense of when I'm about to do something really evil, hastily murmured, 'Pretend, Charlie, pretend!'

Using my fingers as scissors, I pretended. In my imagination I could almost see the great pile of black locks lying all round us on the floor. 'The Philistines are upon you, Samson!'

Once again Robbie struggled to his feet, and this time pandemonium broke out as the Philistines surrounded him and took him prisoner.

'Where shall we take him, Charlie?' asked Susie Forbes, one of the smallest Junior Pilgrims.

I looked around. The hall was full of furniture used for all sorts of different meetings during the week, and in one corner was a pile of folded wooden trestle tables. Ideal. 'Under one of those. We can use the legs as the pillars.'

Elaine interposed, 'I'm not sure that's a very good idea. You mustn't actually tip the table over; you might hurt someone or damage the legs.'

'No, no, we won't!' I assured her. It didn't look very much like the roof of a Philistine banqueting hall, but it would have to do. The feasting Philistines settled down on the floor all round it, drinking imaginary goblets of wine and eating imaginary Eastern delicacies with great gusto.

'Couldn't we have real food?' asked Tom Nicholls, who never missed a chance of something to eat. 'We could just have the stuff we usually have after the service a bit early. It would make it much more realistic.'

Elaine considered this for a moment. 'Well, I suppose it would actually be quite a help to the coffee ladies if we had ours before they come out to serve the adults. All right, Becky, the tray's all laid up in the kitchen, you can bring it out and we'll have it now.'

Becky disappeared briefly and reappeared with a tray of biscuits and squash which were dispensed amongst the assembled company.

'Yum. Nice sheep's eyes,' said Gavin taking a custard cream, and picking up his Bible to check on the next part of the story.

'Bring out the prisoner to entertain us!' he commanded. Robbie managed to crawl under the table, his ankles still tightly tied together, and there he sat, his hands resting lightly on a table leg each side of him.

'You're meant to be blind,' I reminded him, feeling rather regretful that we'd forgotten to act the bit where the Philistines gouge his eyes out.

Obediently, Robbie shut his eyes.

'Now call on the Lord.'

'LORD GOD, REMEMBER ME!' shouted Robbie at the top of his voice, and his face puckered up in a scowl of intense concentration, somewhat reminiscent of a constipated chicken, as he pretended to pull on the two table legs where his hands were resting. The table stood resolutely upright.

It seemed a dreadful anti-climax, somehow, after all that inspired acting. I don't know if it was that, or the fact that I suddenly felt as if I had been made to go to an infants' tea party, but some fiendish inner voice seemed to be telling me to give the whole thing a truly authentic ending.

All it took was two deft kicks aimed at each of the hinges of the collapsible legs, and down came the Philistine banqueting hall.

Robbie must have caught the look in my eye, as he scrambled out in the nick of time, but several of the feasters dropped their squash and biscuits in the panic to avoid the falling table. No one was actually hurt, but there was quite a lot of squealing from some of the younger girls, and the pools of spilt orange mixed with broken biscuits added to the general mayhem, creating a spectacle of which Samson himself would have been justifiably proud.

When we had cleared everything up, Elaine took me to one side for a little chat.

'Charlie, I don't feel you're taking JPs very seriously at

the moment. Don't you enjoy it?'

Feeling a bit guilty, I decided to tell the truth. 'It's not that I don't take Christianity seriously,' I said, 'it's just that I feel much older than some of the others – especially the boys – and sometimes what we do seems so young somehow.'

'But you aren't much older than Robbie or Gavin, only a couple of months. And I don't think your behaviour today was very adult, was it?'

'I know. I can't help it, that's just the way I feel.'

To my surprise, Elaine gave an understanding nod. 'It's really difficult to pitch things right for your age group, some of you are so much more grown-up than others. I think maybe it's time you moved up to Senior Pilgrims. I know you aren't quite old enough, but I think perhaps you've outgrown us. What do you say?'

'Oh, but I couldn't go without Kate and Becky. We were all going to move up together.'

'OK. Leave it with me. I'll talk to Luke Roberts who runs the senior group. He probably wouldn't mind having all of you. But you'll have to behave there, you know.'

I walked home from church with Dad. Unfortunately he had heard about the morning's fiasco from Josh who had been talking to Robbie and Gavin.

'Honestly, Charlie, what got into you?' he asked. This was something I genuinely couldn't answer, but he went on anyway without waiting for a reply. 'Do you realise how much work Elaine puts into running JP's? Not just on Sundays, but mid-week activities as well? I can't think of anyone else in the whole of St Matthew's who cares about the young people as much as she does. I'm really ashamed of you.'

I said nothing; there was nothing to say. I knew he was right about Elaine caring about us. Why else would she put up with me week after week? Most leaders would have given up ages ago. Perhaps things would be better in the senior group.

3

Mon 4th Nov.
Back to school. Noticed a boy I hadn't seen before hanging around with some of Year 11. Must be new. Totally scrumptious – tall, dark floppy hair, grey-blue eyes. Interesting combination. Said nothing to Sabrina; boys never notice me once they've met her.

Our return to school was celebrated with a history trip to Fenchester museum. We went by coach, leaving school at the crack of dawn; not a pleasant experience.

On the whole, school trips are better than lessons, although Mrs Dobson (our history teacher) always manages to make the most interesting outings boring. Fenchester used to be a Roman town, so there were lots of Roman remains that kept being dug up by archaeologists. The best bit was the jewellery, some of it still almost perfect. It was amazing to think that even all those hundreds of years ago there were girls of my age trying to decide what to wear when they went out.

'Did you see that snake necklace?' said Sabrina, as we sat in the coach on the way home. 'I wouldn't have minded one like that myself.'

'I wonder where they went to get clothes and stuff,' I said, yawning; it had been a long day.

'Gamma and Alpha, of course,' said Sabrina, quick as a flash.

'*Where?*'

'Gamma and Alpha. Ancient Greek for C and A. Don't you remember writing out the Greek alphabet in that project on classical civilisations in Year 8?'

I was about to point out that the Romans spoke Latin, not Greek, when a commotion broke out at the back of the bus. Pete Smith and his vile friends always monopolised the whole of the back seat on school outings and sat there eating crisps and singing obscene songs at the top of their voices. The noise today was worse than usual, and it seemed to centre round Fran Cooper who was sitting by herself on the seat just in front of them. I wondered what she had done this time to get them all going: she was one of those people who is forever being laughed at for some reason or another. It was not that she wasn't nice, in fact perhaps that was her trouble, she was too nice; always much too eager to please and to be friends with everybody. The way she looked didn't help either: she could have been quite pretty if she hadn't insisted on wearing those dreadful granny cardigans.

'Fran's got nits!' came a cry from the back of the bus. 'Look! There goes another one! Mind out – it'll jump onto your head!'

'Perhaps she could train them,' suggested another voice, 'Freaky Fran's Fantastic Flea Circus! Roll up, get your tickets now!'

Pete was leaping around the back of the bus, talking to

the palm of his hand in a totally inane manner. 'There, flea, nice flea. You're safe with me, I won't let her put you on show. Here, have a crisp.'

Sabrina turned round in her seat and leant back towards Fran. 'Take no notice, Fran; come and sit with us if you like,' she said, giving Pete and his mates one of her famous withering stares. That's Sabrina for you, all heart.

Fran moved down the bus and sat on the other side of the aisle opposite us. She looked very close to tears. I felt very glad to be sitting by the window, at least I wouldn't have to talk to her. Sabrina chatted to her and me alternately for the rest of the journey. When we got back to school, Pete pushed past us to get off the coach first. 'Mind you don't catch anything nasty!' was his final remark to us as he climbed down the steps. Sabrina made a gesture at his retreating back, the sort of gesture you never see at Junior Pilgrims, but somehow it seemed totally appropriate at that moment.

On Thursday I saw the new boy again, this time coming out of the science labs, talking to one of the girls in his year. He didn't seem to notice me. Not surprising, as Fran was with me; she'd taken to following me and Sabrina around since Sabrina rescued her on the history trip.

'Oooh, Charlie,' she breathed, 'did you see that gorgeous hunk? Wouldn't you like to get to know him?'

I ignored her. Anyone who talks about gorgeous hunks deserves what they get.

Elaine stuck to her word and we had our first taste of Senior Pilgrims that weekend. They usually met on a Sunday night but that Saturday they were having a bonfire party in the vicarage garden. It was all fixed up with

Luke, the leader, that Becky, Kate and I could go, so we were now officially members. Becky was very pleased, especially as the party was going to be in her garden anyway, but Kate was a bit dubious. She was very shy with boys, and some of the boys at SPs did seem terribly grown-up and sure of themselves.

The fireworks were a bit of a disappointment. We'd all contributed a few each, and none of them were very dramatic, perhaps because no one was rich enough to fork out enough money for really good ones. I seemed to remember seeing some really spectacular rockets when I was little; but Kate told me they only looked that way because I was so small. The bonfire was good, though, and the three of us stood and watched it while we ate hot dogs out of paper serviettes, feeling rather out of things. Although we know most of the SPs by sight and some by name, no one seemed to be rushing to talk to us. When Luke came over for a chat, we were very ready to see him.

'So here are the naughty girls who caused so much trouble at JPs,' he said, smiling.

'It was Charlie,' – loyal friend Becky's reply.

'Oh well, whatever. Anyway, who do you know here?'

'Everyone a bit, nobody well,' replied Kate.

'Apart from my brother Tim,' put in Becky. Tim was three years older than her and didn't seem overjoyed at the idea of her joining SPs.

Luke called two or three people over to talk to us. All of them seemed really nice. Luke was really cool too, young, good-looking and very funny, if a bit corny at times. His wife, Debbie, was a brilliant pianist.

When it was almost ten o'clock, Luke produced a carrier bag full of sparklers. Everyone crowded round to get one and we all stood by the bonfire, drawing flashing

30

pictures in the air. As my sparkler died, I suddenly found myself looking across the bonfire straight into a pair of grey-blue eyes.

The new boy from school.

He was looking at me as though he had a vague memory of having seen me somewhere before.

'Don't I know you?'

'We're at the same school. Tatbury High.'

'Oh, right. I've only just moved here and I've met so many new people I can't remember one from another.' He came and stood a bit closer. 'I suppose you've got hundreds of friends at the youth group?'

'Not yet, this is my first time. Me and Kate and Becky.' I pointed at my friends.

'Mine too. First thing my mum did when we moved here was find a church she liked. This is it, so here I am. What's your name?'

'Charlie. Charlotte for long.'

'Mine's Phil. Philip for long.'

Kate was at my elbow wanting me to walk home with her. I smiled at Phil in a kind of see-you-around type way and went to look for the vicar to say thank you for a nice evening. Things were beginning to look up.

Sun 10th Nov.

Went to youth group again in the evening. Luke and Debbie have it in their house, much nicer than the church hall. Had a discussion about gossiping and the effect it can have. Must try harder not to bitch on about people like Fran. Trouble is, it's OK to talk about it in theory with lots of nice Christian people; it's quite another matter when you're there in school and everyone's doing it. Phil was there again, he said hallo, but nothing much else. He tends to stick with the older boys; he left with some of

31

them as soon as the meeting was finished. As we came out of Luke's house they were all hanging around on the other side of the road laughing together. Some of them were smoking, think Phil was one, though can't be sure.

Wed 13th Nov.
Fran turning into the original Klingon. Wherever Sabrina and I go, she follows. I went to the library in my free period this afternoon, I'd only been there two minutes and she turned up and plonked herself and all her books next to me. I was frantically trying to get my English homework done (already two days late) but she kept whispering loudly in my ear until I had to give up. Some of the other people sitting round me actually got up and moved away; if she hangs around me and Sabrina much more, we won't have any friends left.

Dinner time. I was sitting in the classroom with the usual crowd. We'd had to go on a run that morning in PE, and Fran had caused a great deal of amusement by bumbling in miles behind everyone else.

'Not surprising,' sniggered someone, 'anyone that fat is bound to get left behind!'

'Did you see her legs? They go all scarlet and wobble when she runs!'

'And those trainers! I didn't know you could still get them like that!'

'Sh, everybody, not in front of Charlie. She and Fran are great friends.'

'No, we're not,' I quickly protested, mentally saying sorry to God and Luke, 'I can't get rid of her. Can't think why she hangs round me so much; must just be my natural charm.'

Sabrina walked into the classroom as I was saying this.

I didn't know how much of the conversation she had heard, but she gave me a funny look.

This made me feel very guilty, so when the bell went at the end of the day, I made a huge effort and offered to walk to the bus stop with Fran. She was thrilled, of course, and chattered non-stop all the way down the corridor to the main entrance.

'What are you doing this weekend, Charlie? I'm going shopping with my auntie tomorrow afternoon, but I'm not doing anything on Saturday night. Could we get together, you, me and Sabrina, and go to the pictures or something?'

I searched my brain for a suitable excuse, but was saved from making a reply by catching sight of Phil walking towards us, a pile of books under one arm. As we got closer, recognition dawned on his face.

'Hi, Charlie. Going home?'

'Yeah. You? Aren't you going the wrong way?'

'If only. Unfortunately I'm in detention. I've got to stay an extra hour.'

'Why, what did you do?'

'It's a long story. I'll tell you about it sometime – p'raps Sunday evening, if you're planning to be there?'

'Certainly am. See you then.' He walked on.

Fran listened to this conversation, in total silence for once, deeply impressed.

'Charlie, you never told me you *know* him! How did you manage it?'

'Oh, we go to the same youth group at my church,' I said airily, 'I see him all the time,' – this was a gross exaggeration but it sounded good.

'Wow, I wish I came to your youth group!' I could see her brain move slowly into motion, you could almost hear the cogs grinding, and I knew exactly what she was going to say next before she opened her mouth.

'Could *I* come? I *could*, couldn't I? Wouldn't it be great if I came too? We could go together! Just think what fun it would be! Where is your church, Charlie?'

Aagh. My worst nightmare come true. I knew the idea was meant to be that you invite your friends to church, but I seemed to spend all my time trying to put them off. First Sabrina and now Fran.

Eventually I muttered, 'St Matthew's. On the corner of the High Street. But you may not like it. It's all very serious and religious.'

Somehow I didn't think I'd managed to deter her.

I slept late on Saturday morning and was woken from a very complicated dream by Josh and his friend Jamie playing football in the passage outside my room. (Josh had managed to persuade Dad to take them both to the Fenchester Rovers home game today, so they were busy getting in the mood.) In my dream I was sitting on a bus between Fran and Phil and Phil was offering me a cigarette; I knew I had to take it or he would give it to Fran; but when I did, Kate and Becky popped up in the seat behind, shouting, 'The Philistines are upon you, Charlie!' Then they started hitting me with a large hymn-book with loud resounding thumps. I slowly regained consciousness, realising that the thumps were the sound of the football beating against the wall next to my head.

Most bizarre. I staggered out of bed and gave the two boys a piece of my mind.

Josh's obsession with football was getting beyond a joke. Dad was no better, he seemed to encourage it. Mealtime conversations these days revolved entirely round tactics and team formations.

The next evening my worst fears were realised: Fran

turned up at SPs. She spotted me immediately and rushed over to sit in the chair next to me. I'd already warned Kate and Becky about her, so they knew what to expect, but even so, I don't think they were prepared for the great torrent of inane drivel that constantly flowed from her.

'Doesn't she ever engage her brain before putting her mouth in action?' Becky murmured to me, while Fran's attention was briefly caught by the arrival of Phil on the other side of the room.

Luke came over to meet her and welcomed her warmly. 'How lovely that Charlie invited you,' he said, giving me a well-done-brilliant-evangelistic-move look. I looked away.

Phil spied us at that moment and made for our corner.

'Who's your friend, Charlie?' he asked; so I had to introduce Fran, who predictably had an immediate attack of verbal diarrhoea.

'I've seen you in school,' she said, 'you do Physics on a Wednesday morning after break, don't you? I know because I've seen you coming out of the lab, and you always have lunch in H3 with Steve and Mike, and then you play football and your mum drives a white car, doesn't she?'

'Well, yes,' said a bewildered Phil, looking like someone who's just been interrogated by the Secret Police. 'How did you know?'

Fran smiled mysteriously. Such subtlety.

'So why were you in detention on Friday?' I asked him, swiftly changing the subject.

'Caught smoking by the school gates,' he said, grinning, 'I'd've got away with it if I hadn't been wearing school uniform, 'cause none of the teachers remember my face yet; but the blazer was a give-away.'

So I was right, it had been Phil smoking outside Luke's house the other night. I wondered what else he got up to, and wished Kate wouldn't look so shocked.

Sun 17th Nov.
The talk this evening was about forgiveness; Debbie spoke this time and was really good. I could see that Fran was interested, even forgetting about Phil while the talk was going on. There was a time for questions at the end, and hers was the first hand to shoot up. Amazed to realise how little she understands about Christianity. I'm so used to hearing it week after week, it's hard to believe it could all be so new to someone who doesn't go to church regularly.

Wonder why Phil goes to SPs. Somehow it doesn't seem to go with the hard man image. Does it mean something to him, or does he just come to keep the peace at home?

Back at school Fran was worse than ever. She obviously thought that because she had been to SPs we would now be bosom friends for all eternity. Even more gruesome, she insisted on telling everyone else about it.

'I went to Charlie's Youth Group last night,' she proudly informed the class at large, while waiting for Mr Larkin to arrive for our first lesson. 'It was really good – we had this wonderful talk on forgiveness and we sang some brilliant songs. I think being a Christian is really cool.'

I could see Pete Smith's eyes lighting up with malicious interest. I groaned inwardly, and prayed fervently that Mr Larkin would hurry up. Fortunately God answered.

I stopped for a cup of tea with Squirrel the next day

and told her all about Fran. She was very sympathetic, but not very helpful.

'I know people like that,' she said. 'Not much you can do about them. I guess you just have to get on with it. Hopefully this is where being a Christian will make the difference between you and the rest.'

Would she still have loved me if she knew the horrid thoughts I had about Fran? I didn't think I'd risk telling her.

She had other things on her mind that day anyway. She was dying to tell me about her new craze – pottery. She'd just enrolled in classes at the local art college and was taking it very seriously.

'We've been learning how to use the wheel this week,' she said. 'Trouble is, I keep starting big tall pots, and then I do something to spoil them and have to keep cutting their size down. I started three jugs on Wednesday, one after the other, but ended up with three saucers. Still, the decorating is fun. They could always be used for standing plants on or something.'

I tried to imagine her setting up a cottage industry in hand-painted saucers and selling them all at a bring and buy sale at St Matthew's and felt it was unlikely that there would be much of a market for them. Except perhaps among a certain section of SPs who might see them as having ashtray potential.

Back home I went to the kitchen to clean my shoes. Mum was in the hall on the phone to Becky's mum. She was talking in a low voice but not so quietly that I couldn't hear.

'Yes, I know the family you mean. They've just moved in to Dawfield Road… yes, Philip. Or Phil, I think…' My ears pricked up. 'Yes, he's at SPs with the girls, very tall, sporty… no, really? How difficult for his mother…

no, I didn't realise... no, I don't think Charlie has much to do with him... no, well, I'll make sure she... well yes, exactly, you can't be too careful... So how is Tim getting on with his A levels?...'

She came off the phone a few moments later. I stood at the sink, polishing the toes of my school shoes and waited for the onslaught.

'This chap, Phil Riley. You know him from church?'

'Yep.'

'Well, I should be a bit careful about how much you have to do with him. Ann Soames was just telling me that her sister knew his family in the place where they used to live, and apparently he was very wild and got into a lot of trouble. I'm not saying don't be nice to him, just be careful. It's easy to get led astray by someone like that.'

'What do you mean, wild?'

'You know, drinking and smoking and generally doing his own thing. A bit of a rebel.'

I leapt to his defence. 'Just because he's doing his own thing doesn't mean he's going to lead everyone else into a life of drugs and vice!'

'I know, I know. Just be careful, OK?'

I wasn't too bothered. Mum's idea of Wild is an evening out playing Trivial Pursuit with our next-door neighbours.

4

Mon 2nd Dec.
Caught Josh in my room taking all my CDs out of their covers. Said he was looking for my Purple Skies album. Why can't he mind his own business and leave my stuff alone? It's not as if he really likes any of my music, he's just jealous because he hasn't got a CD player of his own. Got my revenge by hiding his football sticker collection.

'Tell you what, Charlie, why don't we have a Christmas party?'

Sabrina was lying full-length on my bedroom floor, idly thumbing through one of Josh's old Beanos.

'Nice idea,' I said, immediately thinking of about a hundred objections. 'Where would we have it?'

'Here, of course.'

Just as I thought. 'Why not at your mum's place?'

'Oh, Charlie, you know our house. There just isn't room.'

'Well, what about your dad's then?' I said, thinking that

sometimes it must be quite convenient to have two separate homes to draw on.

'Can you see him coping with all the organisation? And I'd have to do all the cleaning up afterwards; he's hopeless at that sort of thing. Oh, do say yes, Charlie, it'd be so cool!'

I could already foresee lots of problems. Who would I ask? Just school friends, or church friends as well? The school friends would all expect to be able to drink, and probably hope Mum and Dad would go out for the evening. And what if it all got out of hand? I told Sabrina I'd sleep on it. Perhaps I'd see what Kate and Becky thought.

There was no chance to talk to Becky and Kate that Sunday, but the next evening Becky asked if we would go round to the vicarage to keep her company while she babysat her youngest brother. Her brother was only two; really sweet with gorgeous blond curls and big blue eyes, and so far totally unspoilt. This was probably because he hadn't yet been introduced to the dreaded football – in fact, the perfect brother. Becky's mum and dad had gone out to her sister's parents' evening at her primary school.

We sat on Becky's bedroom floor discussing the party idea and eating toast, while Ben pushed his fire engine round our ankles.

'The problem with having a party at my house is that Mum and Dad have certain ideas about how a party should be,' I said, tickling Ben's toes as he crawled past me.

'Oh, yes,' Becky responded immediately, 'I know the sort of things parents like: charades and memory games and sausages on sticks and everyone goes home at ten-thirty.'

'Well, what did you have in mind, Charlie?' asked

Kate.

'I dunno. Music certainly, and maybe dancing. Just sitting and talking – you know the kind of thing. I certainly don't think Sabrina will settle for party games.'

'The trouble is, would it be just sitting and talking?' said Becky. 'You know what some of those boys are like. And how would your church friends mix with your school friends?'

'Good question. Some of them might be all right – some of them wouldn't. And then there's the booze problem. Mum and Dad wouldn't hear of us having any at all, but some of the boys from school might well try and bring some in.'

'Not just school, if what I hear about Phil is true,' said Kate.

I was about to say something but the phone rang. Becky disappeared to her father's study with pen and paper in hand.

'Brownies want to move the time of their meeting,' she said, reappearing a moment later. 'So, Charlie, what about the gorgeous Phil? Are you going to invite him?' I need hardly say that it hadn't taken Becky and Kate long to work out that I fancied him.

'I don't know. What do you think? He's not exactly a lifelong friend.'

Kate considered for a moment. 'I think you can,' she said. 'After all, you know him from school and home. He's one of the only people you know from both places.'

'And Fran,' put in Becky, smirking in a very unChristian manner.

'Oh dear – Fran!' I said guiltily. 'What am I going to do about her?'

'You'll have to ask her,' said Kate definitely. 'It would

be too unkind not to. Especially now you've brought her to SPs and everything.'

'But I didn't bring her! She brought herself! Do I have to ask her? She'll only spoil everything.'

The phone rang again. Becky made for the door, Ben toddling after her. He had got fed up with his fire engine and was beginning to grizzle. We could hear Becky's side of the conversation, '…Yes, Mrs James, ten o'clock Friday. Yes, I'll make sure he gets the message.'

She returned. 'I think you've got to ask Fran,' she said. 'After all, with lots of other people there, she won't be so noticeable.'

I sighed. They were right, of course.

The doorbell was ringing now. Becky ran downstairs to see who it was, ignoring Ben's rising wails of protest as she disappeared from his view yet again. The door banged and she came back upstairs, staggering under the weight of a huge pile of parish magazines.

'For Sunday,' she said, dumping them on the bed. It must have been a nightmare living in that house with all those interruptions. I couldn't imagine how she ever got any work done.

I didn't feel much the wiser about the party. I would have to bite the bullet and discuss it with the parents.

Tues 3rd Dec.

Sabrina asked if I'd had any more thoughts about the party. She's already planning what she's going to wear. Used delaying tactics. Perhaps the whole thing's a stupid idea after all.

I decided to talk to Dad first; he tended to be easier to handle than Mum. I tackled him while he and I were doing the washing-up together.

'Dad, Sabrina and I were thinking we might have a Christmas party together. What do you think?'

'Yes, great idea. Where would you have it? Sabrina's house?'

'Well, I really thought here, actually; it's a bit difficult for Sabrina at the moment.'

'Oh. Well, I don't think there'd be any problem about that. You'll have to ask your mother, though.'

Typical of Dad that he couldn't think of any problems. Of course, when I brought the subject up with Mum, she could think of hundreds.

'Why with Sabrina? Why not with Kate and Becky? They'd be much more sensible, you know. And how many people are we talking about? What will you eat and drink? Will you play games or what?' I don't think Mum had really got beyond the idea of Ring O' Roses and Musical Bumps.

I did my best to allay her fears and eventually got her to agree to the idea in principle, even picking a date, the Saturday before Christmas. I rang Sabrina before I went to bed to tell her the good news and to check on the date with her. She was ecstatic.

In bed I lay awake for ages, trying to imagine how it could possibly all work out.

I imagined Sabrina, fast asleep, happily dreaming of dim lights, loud music, leather trousers and see-through blouses.

I imagined Mum fast asleep, happily dreaming of jelly, Dead Lions and party bags.

After that, all thoughts of parties were put temporarily on hold as school exams were looming. I began to regret that I hadn't been keeping up with my history notes. It was time for a real blitz on revising and I only had a weekend left. To make matters worse, Josh had also decided that he needed to have a blitz on piano practice. Typical, Mum had spent all term nagging him to practise, and then when he finally did it was at a time when I most needed total peace and quiet. It wouldn't have been so bad if he had been any good, but he hadn't yet progressed beyond tunes with names like 'Middle C's the Note For Me', and 'Up a Space, Down a Space'. Not a very good mix with the beginning of the Nazi party and Hitler's rise to power. Though come to think of it, perhaps if Churchill had sent the troops into battle singing 'Left Hand, Right Hand, Off We Go', we might have won sooner.

On Saturday evening Sabrina rang, suggesting we have a break from the books and go to the big multiscreen Odeon.

'The new Adam Lee film is out this week,' she said. 'It's got brilliant reviews and it's bound to be really good. We'd have to book, though.'

I hesitated for a moment. 'I'd rather go and see the new Jane Austen.'

'What? You can see that any old time. Your mum'd probably even take you; and you'd get in free that way!' said Sabrina, who never missed a chance to get something paid for.

I would have to come clean. 'I can't go to the Adam Lee because it's a Fifteen. You know what Mum and Dad are like.' I knew that Sabrina had no such problems; both her parents thought she was old enough not to be corrupted and had no qualms about her sneaking in under age.

There was a pause, in which she was obviously considering whether to suggest I go behind their backs. Her conscience must have got the better of her as she gave a deep sigh.

'OK, let's do the Jane Austen. Though I think it's a bit ridiculous. I mean, you'll be fifteen next year. Do they think you're suddenly going to turn into a Responsible Adult over night?'

These were my feelings exactly. And they weren't half so strict about Fifteens on television. What was the difference? Still, thank goodness Sabrina didn't put pressure on me to lie to them as some of the other girls at school would have done. In fact the film was excellent, even Sabrina grudgingly admitted to enjoying it. As we were leaving we saw Pete Smith and some of his gang coming out of the Adam Lee film. I quickly pulled Sabrina into the Ladies so that they wouldn't see us. I could do without his comments about Good Clean Family Entertainment.

On the way home we talked about invitations for the party. Mum was very keen that we should send out written ones so that there would be a list to tick off. She likes writing lists nearly as much as hunting for dirty clothes. Sabrina thought written invitations would be very uncool, we should just ask people when we saw them, or over the phone – much more spontaneous. Would I be able to persuade Mum to see it that way? She wanted to know exactly who was coming, which of course depended entirely on who would be going out with who – something I couldn't possibly predict two weeks in advance.

I had more time for last-minute exam revision while Mum, Dad and Josh were out at church in the morning. Mum would have disapproved if she'd seen me working on Sunday, but I'd run out of time after going out to the pictures the day before. I knew Sabrina would have spent the morning working anyway.

Phil was at SPs in the evening (gorgeous new jacket), and I wondered if this was the right moment to invite him to the party. I waited till he was by himself and sidled round to where he was standing.

Deep breath. 'I wondered if you would like…'

'Hallo, Charlie! Hallo Phil!' Drat. Fran was bouncing over, shiny new Bible in hand, all full of the latest exciting bit she had just read. She seemed to have turned into the keenest member of the youth group.

'Did you know that one of the disciples was called Philip?' she said, gazing at him with adoring eyes, obviously very proud of this stunning piece of information.

'Yeah, I knew,' said Philip, apparently not at all irritated by her. 'Actually I think I was named after him. At least him and my great uncle Philip. Charlie was just asking me something; what was it, Charlie?'

'Oh nothing special, just would you like another drink, as I'm getting one for myself?'

Phil looked vaguely bewildered at the offer. 'Uh, no thanks. This fizzy stuff is pretty boring. I'll probably go to the King's Head later with some of my mates.'

Fran's eyes got even bigger. 'But you're not allowed in the pub!' she said. 'You're under age!'

'So?' grinned Phil. One of the older boys was calling to him and he moved away.

'Isn't he terrible?' said Fran, admiringly, when he was out of earshot.

I had to admit, he had a certain sort of style.

It was late by the time I got home. I lay in bed trying to revise until the early hours of morning. Eventually I fell asleep with my book open and the light on.

Mon 9th Dec.
Incredibly tired.
Maths and French exam. Maths awful, French not too bad.

Tues 10th Dec.
English and Geography. Both dreadful.

Wed 11th Dec.
History. All I could think of was 'Left Hand, Right Hand, Off
We Go'.

I read somewhere that you can train yourself to learn
things by listening to music while you study. The idea is
that when you get into the exam, you just think of the
tune and then you automatically remember everything
you learnt while it was playing. Unfortunately it seemed
to work backwards for me; I would think of the topic I
was studying, and then all I could remember were the
tunes I was hearing at the time.

On Friday the thirteenth the exams finished. Sabrina
pointed out the significance of the day's date. Fran
immediately jumped on her and told her off for being
superstitious. She was rapidly taking over my role of giving the Official Christian Line on everything. It was a
nice change to have the pressure taken off me for once.

Christmas decorations were going up everywhere.
They had been up in the High Street for a month
already, and on the last day of exams we put them up in
our classroom. We started singing Christmas carols in
Assembly; the one sort of Christian song that wasn't
generally considered to be totally uncool to know. It was
quite funny, really, to see Pete Smith and co mouthing
'Veiled in Flesh the Godhead see, Hail the Incarnate
Deity'. If they had stopped for a moment to think what

the hymn meant they would have been horrified that such words could cross their lips. I supposed they just thought of it as part of the usual Christmas Thing; amazing how the most hardened types can get all gooey and sentimental with the first flash of tinsel.

The party was only a week away. I would have to invite people over the next couple of days. Mum kept asking me *exactly* who was coming. Sabrina had invited several people, including Fran (serious rapture on Fran's part), so that decision had been taken out of my hands. Sabrina pointed out that I would have to be the one to ask Phil if I wanted him there as she had hardly ever spoken to him. How would I ever find the nerve?

Squirrel came for lunch, as she often did on Sundays. I told her about the party.

'Are you going to dance?' she said, her eyes lighting up. 'I used to dance a lot with your grandpa. You should have seen us jive! Now that was dancing with a capital D, not like the jiggling about you do today. I don't suppose I could come?' she added wistfully.

'No,' I said firmly. There would be complications enough that evening, without her giving jiving tuition to all and sundry. She wasn't at all offended – that was the nice thing about Squirrel, she didn't take things personally.

On Monday the exam results were given out. Mine were not good.

Mr Larkin asked me to stay behind when the bell went for lunch.

'What's happened to your marks this term, Charlie?' he asked. 'They're not so terrible, but you usually do better. Have you been doing a lot outside school?'

'I suppose I have,' I replied, although I couldn't for the life of me think what I had been doing that was so time-consuming.

'Well, what sort of things? Do you play in some team or other, or do you play an instrument?'

'No, neither... I just always seem to be busy.' This was true.

'Well, try and pace yourself a bit better, will you? Are you doing your homework when it's set?'

'Not always.' Hardly ever, in fact. I usually left it till the very last minute.

'OK. Well let's see if you can improve those marks in the summer exams.' No prizes for guessing the next line: 'This is a Very Important Year, you know.'

Of course it was a very important year, it was the year before GCSEs; but that didn't mean everything else was automatically going to stop. I hurried down to join the others for lunch and thought about why my time was so full. I decided it must be because I had a whole extra group of friends and things going on at St Matthew's which other people didn't have. They mostly just had things connected with school. Unless they had some major hobby.

Hobbies made me think of Squirrel, which made me remember that I hadn't thought about Christmas shopping yet. I would have to do it soon.

The next day I was walking down the corridor to the classroom first thing in the morning and walked straight into Phil. I jumped right in with both feet before I had time to lose my nerve.

'Sabrina and I are having a party on Saturday at my house. Do you want to come?'

He smiled. They really were very nice eyes.

'Sure, I'd love to. What time?'

'Eight o'clock. Fifty-seven, Whitelands Drive.'

I'd done it!

5

Wed 18th Dec.
Mum, Dad, Squirrel and I had our annual outing to Josh's
Nativity play at St Matthew's Primary. Couldn't believe it
was only three years since I had left there, everything
*looked so **small**.*

As usual, the school had been hit by the Annual
Christmas Bug and so several of the actors were missing.
Some years it was colds and coughs; this year it was a
rather more dramatic tummy bug. Josh was one of a pair
of Talking Sheep but unfortunately the other sheep had
been sick after lunch and had been sent home. This
meant that Josh had to hold his conversation with himself, as he knew his partner's lines better than anyone
else. Actually, it was quite effective, a sort of dramatic
monologue, like To Be or Not to Be. (Or in this case, To
Baa or Not To Baa.)

Miss Franks, Form Teacher of Class 3, was in charge of
the proceedings, wearing a woolly jumper patterned
with festive snowflakes and a rainbow-strapped guitar

round her neck. The characters included Mary and Joseph, Baby Jesus (acted by a large golden-haired doll), the innkeeper and his wife, the shepherds and their one Talking Sheep, a handful of angels, two kings (number three had also got the bug) and finally a large group of Children From Foreign Lands. This last group was a brilliant idea of Miss Franks, as it used up all the people who hadn't got parts and also meant that children of other nationalities in the school would have a chance to dress up in their own national costumes. Probably the first time Samuel Ogongwe had ever worn full African dress; he usually lived in jogging bottoms, like Josh.

The final scene was the best: the whole cast on stage singing along with Miss Franks and her rainbow guitar, about Christmas being the time for Love and Brotherhood. It was only slightly spoilt by Gabriel falling off the stool where she had been put to look a bit more imposing. At the end they all lined up to take a bow, and Miss Franks came forward to make a short speech.

'Thank you all so much for coming,' she said, 'and I think you'll agree it was a very special evening. And didn't the children all work hard to make it so lovely?'

The proud parents all beamed back at her.

'And now,' she continued, with the air of a conjurer about to pull a rabbit out of a hat, 'now, stand back, children. We are expecting a Very Special Visitor.'

She turned expectantly towards the wings.

From offstage came the thin sound of a tinkling bell. Two small boys appeared, dressed as reindeer in brown jumpers and tights, large cardboard antlers sprouting out of their heads. But something seemed to have gone wrong. The smaller of the two reindeer ran across the stage and whispered in Miss Franks' ear. She nodded and turned back to the audience.

51

'I'm sorry, ladies and gentleman, there seems to be some sort of a hitch. The reindeer are having trouble pulling Father Christmas in his sledge; it seems to be too heavy. The thing is, they have to get it up a steep ramp onto the stage. We have practised this bit, but not with the sledge full of presents,' she added apologetically. Turning to the reindeer again, she whispered loudly, 'Tell him to get out and pull it up himself.'

The reindeer nodded and obediently trotted off to convey this message to Santa.

A minute later he was back. This time we could hear him: 'Jason says he doesn't feel very well.'

Miss Franks tutted impatiently, 'Nonsense. Just stage fright. Tell him all the children are out here waiting and if he doesn't appear in the next five seconds he'll have to stay in at dinner time tomorrow!'

After another pause a small, very green-faced Father Christmas emerged, white beard slightly askew, tugging at a grocery box painted to look like a sledge, loaded with brightly coloured parcels.

'Well done,' said Miss Franks in relieved tones. 'Now, Santa, what have you brought up for us?'

Probably the most unfortunate phrase she could possibly have used, in the circumstances. What he brought up was certainly not what anyone was expecting.

The curtain was hastily lowered. Much the most entertaining evening I'd had in a long time.

Fri 20th Dec.
Last day of term. We played Hangman in the English lesson because all the books had been put away; then played the French version in the French lesson. Wonder what teachers would do on the last day of term if Hangman hadn't been invented.

Every time I think about the party it feels as if a herd of elephants have been let loose in my tummy. Also, I just can't decide what to wear. Sabrina says I should buy a new dress, but I've spent most of this month's money.

In the end Sabrina came with me down to the market after school to help me find something, in the hope that we would find something cheap there. Nothing.

We were just about to give up and go home when her eye was caught by a stall selling beauty products; shampoos, body lotions, shower gel, all that sort of thing. No recognisable brands; it looked like a job lot that someone was trying to get rid of on the cheap.

'Charlie, have you ever thought of dyeing your hair?' said Sabrina, picking up some of the bottles and scrutinising the labels.

I had indeed thought of it, several times. My hair was quite nice, it usually looked quite thick and shiny, but it was the most boring shade of brown.

I peered over her shoulder. 'Do you think they're safe to use?'

'I don't see why not. After all, these days most things have to pass regulations and stuff, don't they? Look at the price on this one!'

It was incredibly cheap. Maybe it was the answer. If I couldn't afford a new dress, perhaps I could at least improve my image with new hair. The label on the box that Sabrina was holding showed a beautiful blue-eyed blonde, tossing her silky golden locks in the sun, and laughing at the world.

'I don't think I want to be blonde,' I said. 'Supposing it goes green. Remember when Denise Luckworth's hair did that?'

'Well, what about red then? It wouldn't be such a

dramatic change. Look, this one's quite gentle, it's more a sort of auburny colour. It'd look as though you just had lovely lights in your hair and everyone would be wondering why they'd never noticed them before.'

I looked carefully at the new bottle she was holding. The girl in the picture looked suspiciously like the blonde on the other label, only this time she was tossing a lovely reddy-brown mane and her eyes were green. I wondered whether they had just coloured the photo rather than used different models. Still, it did look nice. I thought of Phil and imagined him gazing into my eyes, saying, 'Why, Charlie, I never realised what beautiful hair you had!'

I bought a bottle.

I woke on the day of the party, feeling sick with fright.

Sabrina arrived at ten o'clock, bearing carrier bags full of crisps and other nibbles: her mum's contribution to the proceedings. In another carrier bag was a selection of her clothes; I'd decided to wear something of her rather than my own ancient stuff. I spent half an hour trying things on and eventually settled for a little black silky number which was not much more than a slightly lengthened T-shirt. Hopefully it would show off the deep rich tones of my soon-to-be glossy auburn hair.

Dad disappeared into the loft mid-morning and reappeared carrying the Christmas tree. This was installed in the living-room, followed by the usual annual ritual of trying to get the fairy lights to work. Every year is the same: first the lights are tested in their box and always work perfectly. Then they are draped all over the tree; this is the moment when they go on strike. Then comes the long boring business of checking that each bulb is individually screwed in as it should be. Dad switches them on, they still don't work. So he takes them all off the tree again and lays them out on the floor; now they work perfectly. Back on to the tree and try again. Not a glimmer.

At this point he swears very quietly under his breath, then controlling himself with a great effort, calls to Mum, 'I think we really will have to get new lights this year, Helen,' at which point Mum comes through, and with the air of a minor royalty turning on the Regent Street Illuminations, gives the whole tree an almighty shake, instantly transforming the living room into a sparkling Fairy Grotto. Never fails.

I checked that Josh and Dad were occupied with putting the rest of the decorations on the tree and that Mum was busy making food for the party, then retired to the bathroom with Sabrina to create the New Me.

First problem, no instructions in the packet. Just a bottle containing an evil purply-red fluid.

'How much do you think you're supposed to use?' I asked Sabrina.

'Dunno. Suppose you could try just using it like a shampoo. And perhaps you ought to leave it on for a bit between each wash. Give it time to take.'

'OK. Here goes.' I wet my hair and poured the stuff all over my head, massaging it into my scalp. I was slightly unnerved to see my hands stained a deep shade of blackberry, and the suds in my hair were also a strange unnatural pinky purple. Never mind, keep going. I waited a minute or two and rinsed. Peering into the bathroom mirror through the steam, I couldn't tell whether it had had any effect at all. Looking at my hands, you might have got the impression that I had been involved in a particularly brutal axe murder, but as far as I could see my hair was still the same old mousy brown.

'Try putting more on the second time,' suggested Sabrina.

Easier said than done; hair can only hold a certain amount of shampoo at a time. Surplus dye ran in lurid crimson rivers down the basin, splattering the tiles and mirror as it went.

'Do you think that's enough?' I said.

'Yeah, probably. Now leave it on for a bit.'

We sat on the edge of the bath and read magazines for about ten minutes. Then Sabrina looked up at me.

'Charlie! Aaagh! Look at yourself!'

I rushed to the mirror. My hair was still brown, completely untouched by the dye. But my scalp and neck were covered in huge great angry blotches, partly due to the colour, and partly due to a dreadful rash that was just beginning to develop all over my head and round my ears. It started to itch quite horribly.

Outside, in the passage, Josh was shaking the door handle. 'Charlie! Sabrina! What are you doing in there? Can I come in?'

'Go away!' we yelled in chorus.

The next half hour was spent scrubbing at my head with ordinary shampoo, trying to get rid of the stains. The more we scrubbed, the worse the rash got, until eventually it was actually bleeding slightly in a couple of places.

After a bit Sabrina said, 'I think that's the best we can do. You'll just have to dry it now and see how it looks.' She passed me a towel. As I rubbed my head, more dye transferred itself onto the beautiful fluffy white fabric.

I looked up at Sabrina and we both started to giggle hysterically.

'Why, Charlie, but you're beautiful!' choked out Sabrina in an appalling imitation of Phil's voice.

It didn't look so bad once I had used the hairdryer on it, in fact in a dim light all you could see was a sort of a pink glow round the general area of my neck, rather as if I had been sitting in the sun for too long. I thought about wearing a high necked jumper to the party, but in the end decided to brazen it out. I felt very sad about my hair, though. It was still the same boring shade of brown, even if somewhat cleaner than usual.

We went down for lunch. Dad peered at me. 'Have you done something to your neck, Charlie?'

I told him what had happened. I knew it was quite funny but I didn't expect the parents to laugh quite so hard. I sometimes wished they could be a tiny bit more sensitive.

The afternoon was spent organising the room and putting out food and drinks. A lot of arguing had gone on about drink, but eventually I had managed to persuade Mum to make a punch using a small amount of cider.

'It looks so pathetic just to offer orange squash,' I'd said, in one of these arguments over Sunday lunch. 'Some of the boys are sixteen or more, and they're used to drinking beer and things.'

'I know,' said Mum, 'but lots of the girls are only fourteen and are completely unused to drinking, especially the ones from church. Ann Soames would be horrified…'

To my surprise, it was Squirrel who had taken my side. 'I think you should let them have a tiny bit of alcohol, Helen,' she said. 'After all, if they don't learn how to handle it with adults around, they'll never learn the effect it has. Make a punch with just a little bit, and then Charlie won't lose face.'

Good old Squirrel. I could see Mum was still worried,

but she gave in. She also produced lots of bottles of exciting fizzy drinks, at least I thought they were exciting. (I hadn't forgotten Phil's comments at SPs.) I just hoped nobody would bring any booze with them.

It took less time than I'd expected to get everything ready. I brought my CD player and all my CDs down from my room for music. Sabrina had brought hers too so we had a reasonable selection, and Becky had promised to bring a couple as well. We put one on while we waited for people to arrive and gave the room a final inspection. It looked brilliant. One of the good things about having a party at Christmas was that we could just have candles and all the fairy lights on, so there would be no argument with the parents about how dark the room was allowed to be. In fact, it all felt really mellow and Christmassy.

I need hardly say Sabrina looked absolutely devastating, in a miniscule red dress and new silver earrings. I didn't look too bad either, especially in the soft light. Mum and Dad were sitting in the kitchen drinking tea; they'd promised to keep out of the way. Josh had gone round to Jamie's for the night.

I gave a satisfied sigh. Let the festivities begin!

It was fairly awful to begin with, people were so slow arriving and would only talk to the people they knew. For the first half an hour all the St Matthew's people stood at one end of the room, and all the Tatbury High people at the other, with Fran rushing between the two groups like a demented dog caught between two trees. People seemed to warm up over the food, though, and began to be brave enough to chat to new faces. Becky was brilliant at that (must have been the Vicarage training), but Kate was incredibly shy. Sabrina was the star of the evening; you could hardly see her for the crowd of admiring blokes.

One or two nasty moments. Two of the St Matthew's guys got into an argument with a boy from Year 11 as to whether the resurrection really happened or not; the conversation got very heated and I wondered whether to try and break it up, but in the end they agreed to differ and talked quite amicably about snooker.

A couple of lads (Sabrina's friends) from the year above had brought beer with them and one of them had a small bottle in his pocket which looked suspiciously like spirits. I was terrified Mum would see, but I didn't have the nerve to say anything. One of the girls had brought some bottles of alcoholic lemonade, a cunning move on her part, as you had to look very closely at the label to realise they were not just soft drinks. One or two probably had a bit too much judging by the noise they were making, but fortunately Mum and Dad couldn't hear them from the kitchen. The cider cup went down well. I had several glasses myself and was surprisingly witty as a result. What was all the fuss about?

The worst moment was when Dad went into his study and found Denise Luckworth and her new boyfriend entangled in a passionate clinch on his precious swivel chair. He didn't say anything, just gave them his scary I-think-you-would-be-happier-some-where-else look, which was enough to make them leap to their feet, tidy themselves up and come back into the living-room looking distinctly sheepish.

As for Phil, he seemed to be happier with his school-friends, but he talked to everyone and was very friendly whenever we chatted. I noticed him looking oddly at my neck at one point, but he didn't say anything. At least he seemed to be one of the few blokes who hadn't fallen under Sabrina's spell.

Sat 21st Dec.
Think I can safely say the party was a success.

Won't have another one again for a long time, it's far too much hassle.

Very, very tired.

6

Sun 22nd Dec.

Carol Service. The church was absolutely jammed with people and looked totally brilliant, all decorated with holly and candles and a huge Christmas tree. The service started with Josh's friend, Jamie, singing the first verse of 'Once in Royal', unaccompanied, holding one lighted candle in complete darkness. Somebody does this every year but I never get tired of it, there's something very special about the solitary voice in the huge silent crowd of people. It just seems to sum up the idea of the little innocent baby, born to bring light into a world of darkness.

Becky's dad gave a talk on just that idea, and asked if we as Christians were as different from people around us as light is from darkness. That's my problem really. I can't see people as all black or all white – most people are a mixture. And I'm afraid of standing out as too different.

The best Bible reading came last, and was from John 1: the bit that starts, 'In the Beginning was the word'. It was full of such lovely sounding words. It said that although

Jesus had come into the world to bring light to everyone, not everyone recognised who he was. I suppose that means that God is always at work in the world, whether people realise it or not; and his light can creep into the darkest and most unexpected places. And people.

I now had only two days left to do my Christmas shopping. Hoping to avoid the crowds I walked down to the High Street very early on Monday morning to find that the whole town was already a heaving mass of bodies. I didn't really know what to get for everyone so I wandered round for ages looking for inspiration. Finally I came home with the following:

For Dad: Pair of socks decorated with holly and little round disc on the ankle that plays 'Jingle bells' when you press it.

Mum: A paperback cookery book on how to make perfect bread. (Hoped she would take it the right way.)

Josh: A football annual.

Squirrel: A decorated tin for keeping paintbrushes in when she goes to her pottery classes.

Sabrina: New eyeliner she's been wanting for ages.

Becky: Strawberry shower gel.

Kate: A mug saying *Kate* in red letters. (Thought about getting her make-up, but know she won't wear it.)

I wondered whether to look for something for Phil but decided against it. It wasn't as if he was my boyfriend. Anyway, by then I was completely broke.

When I got home Mum was reading through a huge pile of Christmas cards and letters. She always gets loads of those duplicated letters from friends all over the country, full of depressing details about the full and productive lives their families lead. She sighed deeply and read a bit of one out to me.

'…and in the summer George and I organised and spoke at a conference on "Life in the Spirit" which was attended by 600 people. Dominic is head boy and captain of the school cricket team, and Abigail runs her school Christian Union, although she is only in Year 10. One of the twins has got a place in the National Youth Orchestra and the other has just won first prize in the countrywide Maths for Schools competition.' Mum stopped reading and looked up at me. 'What has *our* family achieved this year, Charlie?'

I thought for a moment. 'Well, Dad finally put up the bathroom shelf, didn't he? And you managed to go to at least three aerobics classes before deciding your bum looked too big in a leotard. And there's every chance that Josh may take grade one in the next year or so. And me – well, I was substitute in the Under Fourteens' third netball team earlier in the year.'

'I rest my case,' said Mum. 'Let's face it, we're not quite in the Christmas letter league. Sometimes I feel they only write to us because they're being polite.' She was obviously sinking into one of her sorry-for-herself moods; they usually come on at times like Christmas when she has too much to do.

I gave her a hug. 'You're probably right. I don't know why they bother with you. Shall I help you with mince pies or something?'

Pulling herself together, she hugged me back. 'Sorry Charlie, you're not such a bad daughter. Third netball team is quite an achievement when all's said and done. And at least you haven't got into serious trouble – yet. Yes, mince pies are the next thing on my list, I'll make the pastry and you roll it out.' We spent a happy hour in a warm kitchen, rolling and baking. After a bit, Josh came and joined in too; his speciality was volcanoes made out of cone shaped pieces of pastry, with jam bubbling out of the top like molten lava. They always looked very impressive until he baked them and the jam burnt.

I supposed I was a bit of a disappointment to Mum. I wasn't bad at most things, just rather boringly average. One day I'd amaze her with my brilliance at something, so that she could write Christmas letters about me. Goodness knows what.

I left it till Christmas Eve to wrap up all my presents and put them under the tree. Josh had already put several strange looking packages there. He tended to use nearly as much sellotape as wrapping paper. He had been very secretive over the last few days, locked away in his bedroom for hours at a time. In the afternoon I nipped round to the vicarage with Becky's present and found the place in chaos. Her mum was trying to peel sprouts and talk on the telephone at the same time, her brothers and sisters were all arguing about whose turn it was to wash up, her dad was shut in his study writing his Christmas sermon, and Ben was sitting under the kitchen table screaming blue murder.

'Shouldn't come in here if I was you,' said Becky, 'it's always like this at Christmas. Dreadful time of year.'

I walked away down the road, thinking how disillusioned Mum would be if she could see her perfect family today.

On Christmas Day I was woken at six-thirty in the morning by Josh shaking me with one hand, while clutching a bulging stocking in the other. (Great improvement on last year's five o'clock start.) We jumped on our sleeping parents and climbed into their bed to open the usual assortment of soap, pencil sharpeners, novelty chocolates and satsumas etc. (Every year Father Christmas solemnly takes two satsumas from the fruit bowl downstairs and pushes them into the toes of our stockings; and every year Josh and I solemnly unwrap them and take them downstairs to put them back in the fruit bowl.) This stocking-opening ritual is always the same, as is everything else that happens on Christmas Day.

Dad opened his new socks after breakfast and was very pleased with them, though not as surprised as he might have been, as the minute he touched the parcel they started playing 'Jingle Bells', even before he'd unwrapped them. In fact, the slightest little knock seemed to set them off, so he had to spend the whole day with his feet well apart to avoid accidental contact between his ankles.

The morning service at St Matthew's was very noisy with hundreds of small children. There were loads of people there I'd never seen before, and presumably would never see again. I sat with the family for once, instead of Becky and Kate. This was a mistake, because every time Dad crossed or uncrossed his legs everybody looked in our direction to see where the mysterious muffled jingling was coming from. I saw Phil in the distance with his parents; he waved and was then swallowed up in the crowd. Coming out of church I bumped into a beaming Fran, wearing a white lacy blouse, checked pleated skirt and an enormous pair of dangly Father Christmas earrings. She was clasping a square package which she immediately thrust under my nose as soon as she saw me.

'Happy Christmas, Charlie! Here's your present!'

Seriously embarrassing. Of course I'd got nothing for her.

'Oh, hi Fran, yeah, happy Christmas. 'Fraid I ran out of funds this year so no presents for anyone. Really sorry.

Spent it all on... on... [sudden inspiration] I gave it away! Yes, that's it, I decided instead of giving to my friends this year I would think of those poor people less fortunate than myself. So I gave it all to charity.'

Fran's eyes went all misty. 'Gosh, Charlie, what a really lovely idea. I'm really glad you did that. I wouldn't have wanted a present anyway, if that's what you were going to do with the money. You are a nice person.'

'She is, isn't she!' said Becky, bounding up behind me. 'Look at the lovely shower gel she bought me for Christmas. Thanks a lot, Charlie! Charlie? Why are you looking at me like that? Did I say something wrong? Charlie? Are you in pain?'

Fran's eager face seemed to crumple up in an expression of hurt. She said nothing, but turned and ran off down the church steps into the crowd of departing people. I watched her go, for a moment feeling horribly guilty, and then very cross that she always had this effect on me. I shrugged my shoulders and tried to forget about her.

Squirrel came for lunch and stayed for the rest of the day, also two Nigerian students from the local business college who Mum had invited as they had no family in this country. (I have to say I wasn't very keen about the idea of having two total strangers around, but Mum talked me into it.) One of them was married and had left his wife and daughter behind in Nigeria. It must have been awful to spend Christmas without them. We had all the usual stuff: turkey and roast potatoes and Christmas pudding. Josh got very excitable and rushed round pulling bangers out of crackers in everybody's face.

After lunch we opened the rest of our presents. Squirrel had made something in her pottery class for each member of the family. Josh had a container to keep his football stickers in, I had a little pot for stray earrings, Dad had a tray for paper clips and rubber bands and Mum had a small jar to hold pencils and biros. They all looked strangely similar, although each had its owner's name painted on the side. Squirrel must have felt her offerings were on the small side, because in each pot was a folded five pound note. There were pots for the Nigerians too. Squirrel never forgot anyone.

From Mum and Dad there was money to spend on clothes, from Sabrina a bracelet, and from Josh a huge bar of chocolate. He watched me open it with greedy eyes and then asked if he could have a bit.

In the evening we played a new game that Auntie Val had given the family, which involved making loud animal noises at the tops of our voices. It was quite fun if you didn't stop to think how ridiculous it would have appeared to an onlooker; the Nigerians must have got a very strange idea of a typical English Christmas. Dad and Mum were arguing as to whether a frog went Ribbit or Rivet, when the phone rang. It was Sabrina.

'Hallo, Charlie,' she said, 'just rang to say Happy Christmas and thanks for the brilliant eyeliner.'

'That's OK,' I replied, 'and thank you for the bracelet. Have you had a great day?'

'It was all right,' she said without much enthusiasm. 'I spent most of it with my dad but now I'm with my mum and her boyfriend. I got lots of money and some new CDs. What did you do? And why does your house sound like a zoo?' she added.

'Oh, that's just my dad,' I said. Then, feeling that perhaps greater explanation was needed, put in as an afterthought, 'He's a frog. We went to church and then spent the rest of the day at home.' I could hear one of the Nigerian students mooing and Squirrel squawking like a parrot in the other room. Mum was shouting, 'Charlie! Are you coming? It's your turn!'

'I've got to go,' I told Sabrina, 'I'll ring you tomorrow.'

I felt bad as I hung the phone up, she had sounded very flat. This was only the second Christmas since her parents split up. My family might be weird but at least they're all under one roof. I thought about how strange it must be not to go to church on Christmas Day. It kind of makes the whole thing fairly pointless if you don't spend some time thinking about the meaning behind it all.

On the way to bed I remembered that I hadn't opened Fran's present so I sat on my bed and ripped off the paper. It was a book by Samantha Parkes, the girl who had come last October to talk to Junior Pilgrims about her life on the London streets. Inside the cover Fran had written, 'To Charlie. Thank you for being my friend and helping me to learn about Jesus. Lots of love Fran.'

For some inexplicable reason I felt like screaming.

The house was fairly quiet after Christmas apart from Mum's predictable nagging about thank you letters. I only had two to write, one to Auntie Sue and one to Gramps in Bournemouth, so it was hardly going to take long to do them. Dad took Josh to the football on Boxing Day, not a great success as their team, Fenchester Rovers, were beaten 2-0. Also the weather suddenly turned very cold.

As usual the whole family went to the panto with Uncle Dave, Auntie Val and the three frilly dresses (red velvet at this time of year, with red velvet hair ribbons and black shiny shoes). This year's show was Cinderella. It was only bearable if you decided that resistance was useless and you might as well join in and make an idiot of yourself along with the rest of them. In the middle of the show the audience was divided into two halves, each side led by an Ugly Sister, and made to have a shouting competition.(Oh, yes it is! Oh, no it isn't!) Our side won hands down, almost certainly due to the efforts of our Secret Weapon, Squirrel, who stood up at the end of the row shouting, 'IT'S BEHIND YOU!' in a voice that could shatter glass.

I saw Becky there with her family, high up in the cheapest seats. They seemed to have stopped arguing today and were obviously enjoying themselves. Kate never went to the panto, her parents considered it to be a shocking waste of time; I felt they might well be right. She was going to a modern play by Pinter or someone, which was on at the other theatre. Undoubtedly much more educational.

The year had nearly come to an end, and Luke and Debbie invited everyone in SPs to their house to see the New Year in. I summoned up enough courage to ring Sabrina to see if she wanted to come too, but she was going out to some party with her dad. Fran came, of course. I said hallo to her quickly, and then managed to avoid her for the rest of the time.

It was a fantastic evening. It started with some very silly games suggested by Luke, which got us all laughing hysterically. Then we sat around on the floor trying to outdo each other in telling terrible jokes. As midnight began to come closer Debbie went over to the piano and started playing softly in the background. People got a bit more serious and started chatting to each other in twos and threes. That was when I found myself sitting next to Phil and talking to him about school, and life generally. He didn't seem to like school very much. It turned out that rugby was his passion and that he was dead keen to get into the local team.

'Trouble is, it takes up so much time,' he said. 'My mum isn't very happy about me doing it, because she thinks it stops me getting down to serious study.'

'What about your dad?' I asked, thinking how football brings Dad and Josh together.

'My dad's in the navy,' he replied, 'he's away several months at a time.'

'That must be difficult for you,' I said, trying to imagine living with your dad permanently away.

'You get used to it,' said Phil, looking embarrassed. 'I sometimes think things are easier when he's away. That's why we moved up here, my mum wanted to be nearer to all my aunts and uncles. My older brother is away at college, so Mum and I are pretty much on our own, and she worries about me all the time.'

'You and your mum must be very close then?' I said, thinking about the times I'd seen him hanging around with some of the less desirable types at school and wondering what she thought about that.

'Not really,' he replied, and his voice had a bitter note. 'She's so busy missing Dad, I don't think she has room for any more feelings. So I just do my own thing and don't tell her the bits I don't think she'll like. It's even worse when he comes home on leave, they're like a honeymoon couple, at least they are for the first week or two. Then they usually start fighting. The thing is, she gets so used to running her own life while he's away, she can't cope with him coming home and interfering with the way she does things. Anyway, honeymoon couples don't want sixteen-year-old boys hanging around. I really wish that sometimes we could just live normal lives like other families.' He sighed. 'He's home at the moment for Christmas, as it happens.'

I tried to look warm and caring. It felt good to have him sitting there telling me his problems. But he must have read my face, because he said quickly, 'Hey, I don't need your sympathy. I manage fine.'

I was prevented from saying anything more by the sound of Big Ben striking midnight. We all gathered round in a big circle and held hands, counting the chimes. Luke's radio was tuned in to the celebrations in Trafalgar Square and we joined the London crowds in singing 'Auld Lang Syne'.

Phil stood next to me and held my hand in his.

'Happy New Year, Charlie,' he said, smiling at me.

'Happy New Year, Phil.'

As the party broke up and everyone started for home it began to snow. I ran the short distance home through the snowflakes, singing as I went.

I wondered what the New Year had in store for me.

7

Wed 1st Jan.

Thought about making a lot of New Year's resolutions, such as being nice to Fran and Josh and stuff, but decided the chances of me keeping them was zilch, so abandoned the idea. Still, the New Year does make a good sort of starting point for trying again at life generally and attempting to sort myself out.

There are so many sides to the Real Me. There's the me who is friends with Sabrina who wants to be trendy and amusing and very daring. There's the me who's friends with Kate and Becky, who wants to be a steady, reliable Christian, a support to her friends in times of crisis, and kind to everybody. There's the me who wants to impress Luke and Debbie with my dynamic evangelistic skills and leadership qualities, and yet another me who is terrified of being different from everyone else at school. (I suppose that's the me who's trying to impress Pete Smith and co – hideous thought.) Then there's the me that wants Mum and Dad to be amazingly proud of me, and the me who is trying to be an academic genius to dazzle the teachers. And finally, and of course most importantly, is the me that wants to be devastatingly gorgeous, witty and wonderful whenever Phil Riley is around.

How can all these different people be combined in one human being? It's as if each me is like a new outfit I can put on to impress whoever I'm with. Just so long as no one can see the real me inside – the me that shouts at Josh and is horrible to Fran and is full of nasty thoughts.

It had snowed quite heavily in the night, and on New Year's Day I opened my curtains to find a silent white fairyland outside. Josh was already in the garden when I came downstairs, attempting to build a snowman. Not a very successful attempt. He'd made the base much too small, so it looked more like a snow tower than a snow man. I went and joined him for a bit, but before long the whole thing degenerated into a mammoth snowball fight which ended in the collapse of the snow tower/man. Dad, who is really a small boy at heart, was unable to resist coming out and giving us a short lecture on where Josh's design had been faulty, and then set about demonstrating the right way to go about re-building it. We took no notice of him and carried on pelting each other with snow; to my great satisfaction I managed to get a really large shovelful down Josh's neck. When the snowman was complete, Josh kitted him out as a Fenchester Rovers supporter with scarf and bobble hat. It's a sad team that's so short of fans that it has to rely on snowmen.

By now it was snowing really hard again, so we went indoors and spent the afternoon playing Scrabble with Squirrel who had come over for the Bank Holiday. I curled up in a pile of cushions on the floor and felt very cosy. It was a pity that the holiday couldn't go on for ever.

At SPs that Sunday, Luke talked about New Year's resolutions and new beginnings.

'I wonder how many of us have decided to make a fresh start this year. The thing is, it's no use making lots of promises to ourselves that we aren't going to keep. We all know what happens – we are determined to hold on to our tempers or to be kind to that annoying person; but within a day or two we've forgotten all about it and we're back to where we started.' Amazing, he could have been reading my mind. He went on, 'The important thing is to make a resolution to start the year *with God*; then when these difficult situations come up, we won't be alone.'

That seemed to make sense.

I hadn't seen Fran since the awful moment over the Christmas present, but today it was impossible to avoid her, every time I turned round, there she was. I couldn't bring myself to actually apologise, not because I wasn't sorry, but because it was so embarrassing; so I just sort of tried to include her in the conversation and hoped that we were still on speaking terms. She did seem rather quieter than usual. I was feeling particularly stunning that evening because I had just been to the dentist to have my brace removed. Whenever the opportunity arose I smiled dazzlingly at Phil in the hope that he would see my super new white teeth, but unfortunately he was deep in conversation with Tim Soames and didn't seem to notice me.

Did he like me, or couldn't he really care less whether I existed or not?

The teachers had a staff meeting all day on Monday, so it was Tuesday before we went back to school. The snow had started to melt, making everything very slushy and muddy. The world took on a dismal, dingy feeling, which seemed to seep into the atmosphere at school; everyone sat around listlessly, looking cold and depressed. Everyone except for Sabrina, that is, who had been for a week's skiing with her dad and looked incredibly brown and glamorous. Definitely an unfair advantage over the rest of us. It would have been easier to take if she hadn't been nice as well.

Before we had even got through the first week back, Phil was in mega trouble.

Friday was the one day of the week when the whole school met for assembly in the hall. Proper school uniform was compulsory on these occasions, which for the boys meant blazers and ties. We all had to line up to go in, Year 11 were usually just in front of us, being the next form up.

I was standing in the queue outside the hall talking to a couple of girls from my year, when Mrs Steel (form teacher of Year 11, also known as the Iron Lady for her incredibly severe standards of discipline) came charging past us shouting, 'Philip Riley! Yes you, boy! Come back here!'

I could see Phil just disappearing into the hall. He turned and came back to where she was standing, hands on hips, just in front of where we were waiting.

'And what do you think you are doing, going into assembly looking like that?' she demanded icily.

If I believed in Fate, I would have to say he was rather tempting it. He was wearing jeans instead of school trousers, and a leather jacket over a T-shirt. Admittedly the jeans were the school colour, black, but there was a large rip in one knee. From a great distance you might *just* not have noticed that he wasn't dressed like everyone else, but I doubt it. Certainly not if you had the Iron Lady's X-ray vision.

'Well?' she said, as Phil seemed unable to come up with an instant reply, 'what have you got to say for yourself?'

She was considerably smaller than him, but when she was angry, she seemed to rear up like a poisonous cobra, with little beady eyes that would hold her victim mesmerised as she prepared to strike. Phil, caught in that venomous gaze, was reduced to a nervous mumble.

'I'm sorry, Mrs Steel, I couldn't help it. You see, I was at a friend's last night, and I meant to catch the last bus home but it was cancelled, so I had to stay the night, and I only had the clothes I was wearing. I was going to pop home at lunchtime and change...'

But the Iron Lady was not listening. 'Frankly, young man, I've had enough of your behaviour since you came to this school. You think you can just walk in here and act exactly as you please. Well, you may have been able to behave like that in your old school, but not here at Tatbury High.'

'But what else could I have done! You'd have been even crosser if I'd missed the first lesson.'

'Don't answer me back! Don't you think you're in deep enough water already? I think I'd better put you in detention every day next week. An hour after school in Room 9. Perhaps that will keep you out of trouble.'

Watching Phil, I could see that at that moment his meekness dissolved, as he suddenly lost his cool. 'Oh yeah?' he said, his fists clenched by his sides, 'And who's going to make me?'

'I *beg* your pardon?'

'I said, who's going to make me? Some jumped-up

little teacher with over-inflated ideas of her own importance? I don't think so!'

The silence that fell on the corridor must have been felt all over the school. Mrs Steel pulled herself up to a great height and her chest swelled and heaved. More of a puff-adder than a cobra, I found myself thinking.

'Very well,' she hissed through tightly closed teeth, 'straight after assembly you will go to the headmaster. I will meet you there.' She turned on her heel and marched off down the passage, bristling with rage.

Phil watched her depart. 'Silly old———!' he muttered, kicking the wall. From the way she stiffened her shoulders I think she was still in earshot.

'Will you go?' asked Fran who had been watching with enormous eyes from further down the line.

Phil ignored her. He was heading for the main door of the school.

There was no sign of him in school for the rest of the day. He must have bunked off. I saw him in the evening, though, as I was coming back from dropping a book round at Squirrel's house for Mum. He was hanging around on the street corner with a gang of boys I didn't know. A couple of them were leaning on a motor bike and they all looked quite a bit older than him. They were drinking out of cans and smoking and laughing a lot. I walked past quickly before he could see me.

The next day I met Sabrina for our usual Saturday meander round the shops. She had been at a music lesson the day before when Phil had had his confrontation with the Iron Lady, but she had heard all about it later from the rest of the class. As we walked down the street I told her about seeing him on the street corner the night before.

'Bloke's a berk,' she said cheerfully, gazing at a lovely pair of suede boots in one of the shop windows. 'I don't know what you see in him, Charlie. He could easily have got back home before school yesterday in time to change. If you ask me, he goes out of his way to get into trouble. And anyone who does battle with that old bag is just begging for problems.'

I leapt to his defence. 'But that's what makes him different, don't you see? He's *not* bad, he just doesn't like being told what to do.'

'Well, neither does anyone. But other people don't go round *asking* for trouble like he does. Anyway, I thought he was one of your God Squad lot. I thought they were all supposed to be pillars of the community and stuff. How do you explain that?'

I couldn't. Actually, it was something that had been bugging me for a while. But I still thought he was basically OK deep down. How could he have a smile like that and not be? I heaved a deep sigh and concentrated on suede boots.

He was missing from SPs that week, as well. I suspected he was out with the motor bike lot. Fran was there of course. She seemed to have forgotten about the Christmas present business, and was bursting to tell me her latest piece of news.

'Guess what, Charlie! I saw Mr Carter yesterday morning coming out of Phil's house!' Mr Carter was deputy head and teacher in charge of pastoral care and discipline. I decided to refrain from asking Fran what she was doing hanging around Phil's house on a Saturday morning.

'And?'

'Well, he must have gone in to talk to Phil's parents; he was there for ages.'

I wasn't sure if this was good or bad. 'Oh well, I expect he sorted him out,' I said, in a very couldn't-care-less kind of voice.

'What, Mr Carter sorted Phil out, or Phil sorted Mr Carter out?' giggled Becky, who had been listening to the conversation with interest.

'Bit of both, probably,' I yawned. I hoped he hadn't been suspended or anything. But surely not, he was only a bit rude to a teacher. People had done far worse than that and lived to tell the tale. Even drugs and stuff. Though of course there was the little matter of him bunking off when he was supposed to be seeing the head. And the fact that he was caught smoking on school premises last term. And probably several other crimes that I didn't know about.

At the end of the evening Luke asked if anyone knew where Phil was. I decided it was better not to mention having seen him with the older boys and said nothing.

To my great relief, he was back in school on Monday. I saw him going to the detention room as I was going home, presumably Mr Carter was letting him off with his original punishment. But somehow I didn't get the feeling he had turned over a new leaf.

I hadn't seen Squirrel for a few days, so I stopped off at her house for a cup of tea. She had a terrible cold and looked awful, with red nose and watery eyes. I noticed for the first time that she was beginning to look quite old. The pottery craze seemed to be on the way out; she had just bought an old set of bagpipes at a car boot sale and was trying to teach herself the basics. The resulting noise closely resembled a cat being slowly tortured to death. Fortunately, most of the time she couldn't get enough air into the bag to get out any noise at all.

'It's no good, I think I'll have to take lessons, Charlie,' she said, sinking in a pale and exhausted heap into an armchair. 'There must be a knack to it. Perhaps you could look out for a Teach Yourself Bagpipes book, next time you're out shopping with Sabrina.'

I agreed that I would, although I didn't somehow think it was the sort of thing one was likely to find in the average high street shop.

'So how are things at school?' Squirrel asked, once she got her breath back. 'Nice to be back?'

'Delightful,' I replied. (We'd just been studying irony in English.)

'How's things with Fran?'

'Could be worse. I've got problems with another friend at the moment, though,' I said, choosing my words carefully. 'There's someone at school in the year above me who also goes to SPs, who keeps getting into trouble with the teachers. I don't think this person is bad, more misunderstood really, so is it wrong to want to hang around with them?'

'Not necessarily. As long as you're careful not to get led into doing things that you're uneasy about. In fact, perhaps friendship from you is just what she needs.'

'It's not a she, it's a he,' I said, as casually as I could.

'Oho, it's a he, is it?' said Squirrel. 'Now, all becomes clear. Well, in that case I should be extra cautious. It's always harder to resist being led astray if the one doing the leading is a bit fanciable.'

'It's not like that at all,' I protested, 'I don't *fancy* him. I just like him.'

'And I'm the Queen of Sheba,' said Squirrel, laughing. 'All right, have it your own way, Charlie. But do be careful.' She sneezed an enormous wet sneeze into her big white hanky.

'And anyway,' I continued, 'it's not as if he ever talks to me, except just as someone he sees about the place. So the chances of me being led astray are tiny.'

Back at home I found Josh in my bedroom, rifling through the drawer of my desk. There were letters and papers everywhere.

'*What* are you doing?'

'Jus' looking for some glue,' he said guiltily. 'Got to stick some pictures in my geography folder.'

I put on my most menacing face. 'Listen to me, Josh Hudson. If I ever find you in my bedroom again, I'll take all your football mags and stuff them down the loo. Get it?'

'No you won't, cos I'll hide them! Anyway, I know all about you now! I know that you fancy Phil Riley!' He pointed to Phil's name scrawled in my handwriting on the cover of an old rough book at the top of a pile of papers.

'Just get out of here, now!' I yelled.

He ran off downstairs, chanting, 'Charlie fancies Phil, Charlie fancies Phil! Charlie and Phil, sitting up a tree, doing what they…'

'Get lost!' I screamed after him.

Nothing was sacred in my family.

Wed 15th Jan.

Think I've caught Squirrel's cold. Feels as though someone's been charging up and down the inside of my throat in running spikes.

Fran being particularly irritating at school. Insists on talking nineteen to the dozen, but has absolutely nothing interesting to say. Takes all my willpower not to hit her. Why does Sabrina never lose her temper with her?

Weather is freezing cold. Snow has gone, but icy wind and sleet instead, and permanently grey skies.

81

Kate rang, feeling very depressed. Parents threatening to stop her from coming to St Matthew's, they think she's getting too narrow-minded about religion. Funny old world, where some parents try to force children into going to church against their will, and others try to stop them from going.

Fran had caught the cold as well, which was not surprising seeing how often our paths crossed. She sat behind me in English and kept sniffing very loudly in my ear. To his delight, Pete Smith caught her wiping her nose on her school jumper.

'Mm, tasty. Got anything nice up there, Greensleeves?'

I tried very hard not to laugh.

Later, I passed Phil with two of his mates in the corridor on the way to PE. He didn't seem to recognise me at first, but then he said, 'Oh hi, Charlie. Haven't seen you for a bit.'

'*I*'ve been around. It's you who's been missing. Coming to SPs on Sunday?' (Keep it dead casual.)

'I might. Depends on how busy I am,' he said, non-committally. As he walked on down the passage I heard one of his mates say, 'What's SPs, then, Phil?' I couldn't hear his reply, but he must have made some clever wise-crack, as all three of them burst into unpleasant laughter. Really, I could do without Phil Riley.

On Saturday Luke and Debbie organised an impromptu outing of SPs to the bowling alley. It was good fun. I scored three strikes and beat Becky who is usually the champion on these occasions. We stopped off for a coke at McDonalds on the way home. We must have seemed a very rowdy group, spreading ourselves over three or four tables and generally making a lot of noise. Kate had been allowed to join us as it was a purely social event and, surprisingly, Phil came on the outing too. I would have thought he might have been some-where else on Saturday night, but he seemed to enjoy being with us and bought a large bag of chips which he ate sitting beside me, Becky and Fran.

'Didn't think we'd see *you* on a Saturday night,' Becky said to him, in between noisy slurps on a straw. 'Nothing better to do?'

Phil grinned. 'Not today. Might not make tomorrow evening, though.'

'Why not? Afraid of what your mates might say?' I enquired nastily, remembering how he had laughed with his friends.

He looked slightly ashamed. 'Look, I'm sorry about yesterday, it's just that it's not very cool to go to a church youth group with a load of teeny-boppers from Year 10. I'm sure you understand.'

I understood only too well, but I wasn't going to let him get away with it. 'So you'll come and do things with us, as long as nobody knows you're doing it. Is that right?'

'No, of course not. Look, it'd be OK if it wasn't a church thing, it's just that most people's image of church youth clubs isn't very good. Ping-pong and sitting round singing Kum Ba Yah with leaders who wear beards, socks and Jesus sandals. I know they're wrong, but that's how they see it.'

I glanced across McDonalds at Luke who was looking particularly delectable in a green rugby shirt, old pair of jeans and scuffed brown boots. No beard there, although a certain amount of stubble round the general chin area. He didn't play the guitar either, much to the amazement of older members of the congregation who assume that *all* youth leaders play guitars.

'Luke's not a bit like that,' I pointed out.

'Well, surely it's up to people like you to change the image, Phil,' said Kate, who had been quietly listening to the discussion from the end of the bench.

'OK, OK you've made your point. Look, I'll tell you what. Just to show that I'm not ashamed to be seen out with you, why don't you all come out with me and my mates to the pub tomorrow evening?'

There was a silence.

Becky said quickly, 'We couldn't. For a start, we're under age, which incidentally so are you, and none of our parents would let us. And anyway we've got a visiting speaker at tomorrow night's SPs, and we couldn't possibly let Luke and Debbie down. Sorry, Phil.'

But Phil was not to be put off. 'OK. So what about you, Kate? Do you want to come?'

Kate blushed. 'Oh no, no, I'm not allowed out on Sunday nights now anyway. Not me.'

'Charlie? Surely you're not afraid to have a bit of fun? You've always struck me as a girl with a bit of life. Are you coming?'

I took a deep breath. Mum and Dad needn't know, they'd think I was at SPs. And this might be my opportunity to get closer to Phil and to be the friend he so obviously needed. And going to the pub wasn't a huge crime, loads of my friends did it. It's not as if I was planning to get totally smashed or anything, just to have a friendly evening with a few mates. What would be the harm in it? And he'd said I struck him as a girl with a bit of life. That was definitely a compliment I couldn't pass over.

'OK. Cool. Where are you going?' I could feel Becky and Kate staring at me in shocked disapproval, but took no notice.

Fran was also staring at me, but with a mixture of envy and admiration. She turned to Phil and burst out, 'I could come too! I'll come with Charlie!'

The nerve of the girl.

'Great,' said Phil, without batting an eyelid. 'We'll be at the Leather Bottle from eight o'clock onwards, you can just come in and find us.' He turned to me. 'What about your friend from school – Sabrina, isn't it? Do you think she'd like to come as well? I reckon one or two of my mates would really like her.'

'I'll ask her,' I said, but not very enthusiastically. I always felt plain and unexciting next to Sabrina. Still, I supposed it would be nice to have her around for moral support.

Luke came over from the next table. 'What are you guys so deep in conversation about? Planning a revolution or something?'

'Just social arrangements,' I said, guiltily.

'Right, well could you socially arrange to hurry up? It's time we got you all home.'

I sat between Kate and Becky in the minibus on the way home. Neither of them said much, so I made bright and sparkling conversation about the scenery. As soon as I got back I rang Sabrina.

'Phil and some of his mates have asked us out for a drink tomorrow evening. Do you want to come?'

'What, in the pub?' said Sabrina, sounding very surprised. 'You'll get chucked out if anyone spots you.'

'I know, I know. Look, Breeny, this is my chance. Phil may never ask me out again. Are you coming or not?'

'Won't I be a gooseberry?'

'Please try and follow the conversation, will you?' I said patiently. 'It's not just me and him, it's lots of us. He wants you to come and meet some of his friends. Well?'

'Well, all right,' said Sabrina dubiously, 'but don't be surprised if we get into trouble.'

'I'll meet you at eight-thirty outside the Leather Bottle. I'll have to go to the evening service first, but then I'll come on.'

'Doesn't your youth group meet on Sunday evenings after the service?'

'Yes, but I'm going to give it a miss tomorrow. I'll see you then.'

'OK. But I hope you know what you're doing. See you.'

Sun 19th Jan.

Woke up with a bad feeling in my stomach. Not usually in the habit of lying to the parents, and the idea of it feels horrid. Still, perhaps I'll be a helpful influence in Phil's life, and although Mum and Dad might not approve of my methods, they would surely support the motives behind them.

Squirrel came for her usual Sunday lunch visit and made me feel a hundred times more guilty by asking all about the visiting speaker who was coming to SPs. I was able to tell her all about him, as Luke had given us the low-down last week. I didn't actually say I would be there, but I felt dishonest just the same. It's even worse deceiving Squirrel than the parents – she's always so straight and

87

expects everyone else to be the same.

I thought quite hard about what to wear on an evening out at the pub with Phil, and eventually settled for a skirt I had bought with my Christmas money, with a skinny black jumper. It was important to look mature and sophisticated. As I put them on I remembered what I'd written in my diary on New Year's Day about putting on an image like a set of clothes. What was the image that I wanted Phil to see? Was it really such an attractive outfit?

It was very difficult to concentrate on the evening service. Finally it came to an end, and while people were moving out to the hall for coffee, I grabbed Fran by the arm and pulled her out through the side door.

'Come on! Before Luke or someone asks us where we're going! Or Becky stops to give us a lecture!'

We walked quickly down the road and into the High Street. To get to the Leather Bottle we had to go through the main shopping area, spookily quiet and deserted on a dark Sunday evening. Two tramps were sitting in the doorway of Boots, a bottle of whisky on the pavement between them. One of them held out a hand for money as we went by, spluttering out a string of swear words as we hurried past.

I was relieved to see Sabrina outside the pub as we got near. She was stamping her feet up and down in the cold and looking fairly fed up.

'Come *on*,' she said, opening the door, 'I'm frozen.' The Leather Bottle wasn't like the King's Arms, where Dad and Mum sometimes took us for lunch as a treat at the weekend. It was brightly lit, smoky and very hot, stuffed so full of people that you could hardly move. They were mostly in their late teens and early twenties. I looked round desperately for Phil, and at first thought he must have decided not to turn up, then I saw him right in the opposite corner, surrounded by a group of the boys I'd seen him with the day he'd bunked off school.

'Over here, girls!' he called. Fran, Sabrina and I pushed our way through the heaving sea of bodies, trying very hard to look as though we were eighteen and came in here every day of our lives.

'Thought you wouldn't come,' he said regarding us with an amused smile. He waved his hand at his mates. 'Don, Spike and Al. Sabrina, Charlie and Fran.' Easy to see where Spike had got his name, with greasy black hair sticking out in all directions. He was looking at Sabrina as if he would like to eat her. Al looked at least twenty and wore a T-shirt with a skull on the front. Don looked a bit younger and more like Phil.

'So, what'll you have?' said Al, once we were all sitting down.

This was a problem. What was the thing to ask for? Phil was drinking beer, that was fairly straightforward. The other guys had different drinks, none of them recognisable, but I suspected they were all spirits.

'White wine, please,' said Sabrina, apparently totally at home with the situation.

'Yes, I'll have the same,' I said, relieved to be able to copy her, although I didn't really like wine very much.

'OK. And Fran?'

'Oh, I'll have an orange juice,' said Fran. 'I don't drink.'

Al laughed in an unpleasant told-you-so kind of way, but Phil just raised his eyebrows. 'Two white wines and an orange juice,' he said to Al. Turning to us he added, 'He'll get the drinks. They might ask me for ID if I go.'

I took two or three big gulps of wine as soon as it arrived and began to feel much more relaxed. After all, this was no big deal. Most of my schoolfriends drank quite a lot at parties and places, and none of them were alcoholics. I was tightly wedged between Phil and Don, with Fran sitting opposite. Sabrina was next to Spike, who was looking at her in a very suggestive manner. I could see her pulling her skirt lower down her legs and wriggling her stool as far away from him as possible.

'Fag?' said Al, holding out a packet of cigarettes. All the boys were smoking. Sabrina and Fran shook their heads but I thought: in for a penny, in for a pound, and helped myself to one. It took several attempts to light; I couldn't seem to suck at the right moment.

Feeling slightly sick, I turned to Phil. 'So how are things? Has your Dad gone back to sea yet?'

'Yeah, he went last week. House is quiet, but Mum's all misery again.'

'Have you managed to persuade her to let you try for the rugby club?'

'No. I've been in so much trouble at school this term, she thinks it'd just be another distraction. It's not just the matches, it's all the training they do as well.'

I knew he had taken mock GCSEs at the end of last term, so I asked, 'How did you do in your mocks?'

He made a face. 'Don't ask.'

The cigarette made me cough so much that I drank the wine rather faster than I intended and the glass was already nearly empty. Spike went to the bar this time to order more drinks. Sabrina was still sipping her first glass of wine, and Fran had hardly touched her juice. I suddenly realised I would not have enough money to buy a round, and maybe it would be expected of me.

'About money…' I said, but Phil brushed the problem aside. 'It's OK, these guys are rolling in it. They can afford to buy your drinks.' I wondered how they managed to be rolling in it. Presumably they all had jobs, or perhaps they were on the dole. Certainly weren't still at school.

Sabrina pushed Spike's hand off her knee.

After this things get a bit blurred in my memory. I began to be tremendously charming and witty, and felt that I must be making a stunning impression on Phil, with my constant flow of hilarious one-liners. I was vaguely aware that when Sabrina wasn't fighting Spike off, she was watching me with a less than admiring expression.

'What's your problem?' I asked, but she simply shrugged her shoulders.

Spike and Al kept offering to refill my glass. After a bit I realised that I had probably had enough, so I asked for coke. They exchanged smiles and returned with my request. Obviously they weren't the sort of blokes who would get a girl drunk.

The only fly in the ointment was Fran who kept chatting away ad nauseam to Phil about school and which teachers she liked and didn't like.

'Mrs White's OK. She's Home Ec so I don't suppose you have her, do you?'

'No,' said Phil.

'Mr Larkin, have you had him for History? He always wears very colourful ties.'

'Really?' said Phil.

'…And then there's Mrs Franks who takes us for geography, she's really nice, and we had some very interesting lessons on rock formation. She showed us these brilliant photographs of carboniferous limestone…'

I could stand it no longer.

'Pack it in, Fran,' I said. 'Have you any idea how boring you shound?' Strange. Something funny seemed to have happened to my voice

Fran looked hurt. 'I was just telling Phil…'

'Well, don't, OK? Nobody'sh intereshted. I mean intertested. Who wants to talk about school now?' Why did my head feel so strange and fizzy?

'Leave her alone, Charlie,' said Phil. 'She means well.'

'No, she doesn't,' I said, speaking very carefully so that the strange lump under my tongue wouldn't get in the way of my words. Although I could hear the words I was saying, I didn't seem to have any control over what came out. 'She's out to get you. She really fanciesh you and she thinksh that by spouting all that drivel she's going to make you fancy her. What a joke!' I laughed ironically to drive the point home.

'Charlie,' said Sabrina warningly.

The room was whirling round in a very interesting manner, but still I went on, warming up to the subject as I went along.

'Everyone in school thinks she's a freak. Nobody wants to sit next to her for anything. Every time she opensh her mouth, shomething shtupid comes out. She's fat and shpotty and her clothes are beyond the pale. And the thought of her with Phil!' Indeed the thought of her with Phil was too gross to contemplate. 'Beauty and the beasht! Except in this case the Beasht is female!'

I thought Sabrina was trying to say something to me, but her voice seemed to be coming from a distance. My stomach was churning in the most alarming way. Perhaps I was at sea. Phil's friends were grinning broadly and nudging one another.

'Did you put something in her drink?' came Sabrina's voice from across the waves, but I couldn't catch the reply.

'Beauty and the Beasht,' I repeated, delighted with the joke.

Fran's face floated into my line of vision. She had leapt

92

to her feet, and even in my zombified state I could see her ashen face and eyes brimming with tears.

'I hate you, Charlie Hudson,' she said very quietly, 'and if you're what a Christian is meant to be, then you can keep your stinking Christianity! Sabrina has been a much better friend to me than you could ever be capable of, in spite of the fact that she isn't one of your God-loving lot. And don't worry, I won't bother you ever again!'

She squeezed between the tables and made for the door. Sabrina immediately got up to follow her.

'Good,' I said, to no one in particular. I was just about to say something else profoundly clever when I realised that the barman was heading in our direction, presumably drawn by all the noise.

'Oi, you lot,' he said, 'how old are you? You. You're under age, aren't you?' He was pointing at me.

'I might be,' I said, for some reason unable to stop giggling. 'What age am I meant to be?'

'Out!' he said. 'All of you, out! Take your friends and go. Do you want me to lose my licence? I must say, young lady, if I was you I'd be more careful about who I hang about with. Go on, out! And if you don't want me to take further action, don't come back!'

I staggered to my feet. The sea was roaring all around me now, and my insides were lurching about like a giant roller coaster. I took a step.

Blackness.

9

I came round very, very slowly, like someone regaining consciousness after a long operation. At first I was only aware of light and the sound of distant voices, then I began to notice that the room was filled with an enormous beating throbbing sensation. As the darkness began to recede, I realised that the throbbing was actually inside my head. The memory of a scene in the cartoon version of Snow White floated through my brain, where the seven dwarves are working away with their pickaxes in the mines. I decided that all seven dwarves were now relocated inside my head, chipping away at my skull, singing a cheery tune to keep themselves in time. Heigh ho, heigh ho…

Where was I? I had no recollection of going to bed. Very carefully, I opened my eyes. My clothes were all neatly piled on the chair next to my chest of drawers, my black skinny jumper and my new skirt. Something stirred in my memory, but I couldn't get hold of it. I had a feeling that I had done something terrible, but I couldn't for the life of me remember what. Somewhere downstairs I heard Josh's voice calling, 'Mum! Where are my football boots?'

The sound of his voice seemed to send the seven dwarves in my head into a further frenzy of effort. I imagined them chipping away at the rock which was my skull, chiselling away at layers of shale, sandstone, limestone, granite… hang on, limestone… carboniferous limestone… Fran and geography lessons…

Suddenly, disjointed memories of last night started to flood back into my brain. Oh no. I couldn't have said that. Not in front of Phil, I must be imagining things. Surely I couldn't have made such a fool of myself. Even I wasn't that stupid. As the whole nightmarish episode began to filter back into my memory, my tummy gave a tremendous heave. I flung aside my duvet and dashed for the bathroom. Only just in time.

I staggered back to bed and lay there, a cold, sweaty, groaning heap. The pain in my head was even worse, and from somewhere came a terrible smell of stale tobacco. How had I got home? The last thing I could remember was trying to stand up, when the barman chucked us out. Someone must have got me home and put me to bed. And how had I got into such a state so quickly? I knew I'd had a couple of glasses of wine, but surely they weren't enough to have such a devastating effect? And after that hadn't I stuck to coke?

The door opened quietly and Mum stuck her head in.

'Are you awake, Charlie? How are you feeling?'

'Totally gross,' was all I could get out.

Mum came and sat on the bed. She looked very tired. 'Charlie, Dad's already gone to work and I'll have to go too in a few minutes, so I'm going to have to leave you here alone. Do you think you'll be all right?'

Silent nod. I couldn't trust myself not to throw up again if I opened my mouth.

'I've rung school to tell them you're not well, so they're not expecting you today. Squirrel will pop in later in the day to make sure you're OK. I should just lie still for the morning if I were you. Does your head hurt?'

I nodded again.

'I'll give you a couple of painkillers. Try to drink as much water as you can, you've probably got dehydrated.' She paused. 'Charlie, I don't have to tell you how disappointed I am in you. I know it's tough for you, trying to hold on to your faith without becoming a boring little goody-goody, but I think this time you've gone too far, don't you?'

I said nothing. I was hoping she would go before I started crying.

'Well, we'll talk about it later. You sleep for now.' She stood up and went to the door.

I summoned up my strength. 'Mum?'

'Yes?'

'How did I get home?'

'Sabrina brought you back, and Phil Riley helped her. At least he had the decency to do that, although I imagine it was him who got you into such a state in the first place. I did warn you about him, Charlie.'

She brought me a couple of painkillers and then I heard the front door slam as she left for work. I fell into an uneasy sleep, full of vivid dreams.

At midday the phone rang. I dragged myself out of bed and stumbled to my parents' room to answer it. It was Sabrina, phoning from school in her lunch hour.

'Hallo, Charlie, are you OK?'

'Just about,' I replied. My head was easing up very

96

slightly. 'What happened?'

'You passed out,' said Sabrina. 'I thought you might be feeling dreadful, so I came back after seeing Fran home, in case you needed me. You were in the ladies' toilets and Phil and the barman were throwing cold water over you. The other guys had scarpered, needless to say. For a bit I wondered whether we ought to take you to the Casualty department at the hospital, but once you were conscious the barman thought it would be all right to take you home.'

It was difficult to take all this in. 'Did I walk home?'

'I think walk would be a bit of an overstatement. You had an arm round both me and Phil, and we virtually carried you. You were singing most of the time. You should have seen your dad's face when we rang the doorbell.'

I could imagine. 'How did I get so drunk? I didn't have all that much more than you…'

'I think those repulsive friends of Phil's were responsible. I've seen it happen before. They buy you a soft drink and then slip something in it when you're not looking. Probably vodka – it's very strong and hard to detect if you've already had a couple of drinks. That Spike guy was a *slimeball*.'

That would explain it. I think I had two or three cokes, so if each one had been spiked – of course, that's where he got his name – no wonder I had ended up on the floor.

Sudden thought. 'Did they do Fran's drink too?'

'No, I think they thought she was too easy a target. They picked on you because you were so obviously trying to be cool and make an impression on everyone.'

The next question was hard to ask. 'Have you talked to Fran today?'

'No, she's not in school. She was pretty upset last night, you know, Charlie, and I can't say I blame her.'

No answer to that.

'What about Phil? He must think I'm a complete prat.'

'That just about sums it up,' said Sabrina, remarkably unsympathetically. 'I think he feels a bit guilty for inviting you to come, but after all you're a big girl now and you've got to be responsible for your own life. He was pretty shocked by the things you said to Fran. Drunk or not. You do remember what you said, don't you?'

Unfortunately, I did. At least, up to the moment when I blacked out. Perhaps I'd said even worse things later.

'Well, I must go now, we've got a hockey practice over lunchtime. Hope you feel better soon.'

She rang off.

I put the phone down and sat on Mum's bed, staring into space. Sabrina had sounded very offhand. I thought it was unlikely she would ever want to talk to me again. Nor would Fran. Nor would Phil. Nor would Mum and Dad. Did I have any friends left?

I heard the sound of the front door opening and someone coming into the hall.

'Who is it?' I called. Perhaps the friendly neighbourhood serial killer come to put me out of my misery.

'It's only me, Charlie!' called Squirrel's voice.

I teetered downstairs to find her, and was immediately enveloped in an enormous hug.

'Poor old Charlie!' she said, squeezing me tightly. 'What a state you've got yourself into! Come on, let's go and make a cup of tea.'

The tea was like a magic potion from heaven. We sat together at the kitchen table and I told her everything that had happened. She listened to the whole sorry story without a single word of criticism, then took my hand.

'You poor darling,' she said, 'what a hard way to learn a lesson. And now I suppose you feel as though everyone hates you?'

Dead right.

'It'll pass,' she said. 'It may take a little time, but after a while people will forget. It may be difficult going back to school if you're the number one subject for gossip, but you'd be surprised how quickly people get bored with a topic and move onto something else.'

'Even Fran?' I said. 'Will things ever be normal between me and Fran again?'

'Ah well, you may have to work on that one,' said Squirrel. 'There's no doubt that you owe her a big apology. It may take a while to repair things with her. Are you willing to try?'

I thought hard. 'Yes, I am. Though goodness knows how.'

'Perhaps you'd better have words with God about it,' said Squirrel gently. She never rams God down my throat but he's always there in the background when she's talking to me. I nodded.

'Thought as you were feeling a bit delicate you might like some soothing music,' she said, changing the subject, 'so I brought my bagpipes round.'

Horrified, I opened my mouth to protest, then caught sight of her twinkling eyes.

'Only joking.'

I spent the rest of the day recovering. I expected a major lecture when Mum and Dad came home from work, but Squirrel must have been talking to them, as they said very little about yesterday's fiasco and just carried on as though nothing had happened. However, I didn't feel I was exactly flavour of the month.

By the next morning I had recovered enough to go back to school although my face in the mirror still looked a bit pale and interesting, and I had developed an aversion to sudden loud noises. The fears that I would be the number one subject of gossip seemed to be groundless, amazingly no one seemed to have heard about Sunday evening. Perhaps I was being incredibly naive, maybe people got legless every day of the week and nobody bothered to mention it. Or perhaps Sabrina had just been unbelievably discreet and said nothing. Fran was still off school, so she couldn't have said anything to anyone.

Mr Larkin took the register as usual in the morning. When he got to my name he looked up and said in a very normal voice, 'Glad to see you back, Charlie. Feeling better?'

I mumbled, 'Yes thanks,' and looked furtively round the room to see if anyone was sniggering, but no one seemed at all interested. Pete Smith, never one to miss an opportunity to slag off a fallen saint, was behind his desk lid, drooling over one of his highly dubious magazines with one of his mates, ignoring the rest of the class.

It wasn't until break that I had an opportunity to talk privately to Sabrina.

'Have you said anything to anyone about Sunday night?'

'No, why should I?'

'Well, I just thought…' What did I think? That Sabrina would get a kick out of gossiping about me with the rest of the class? Would I do that to her? But then she would never have got herself into such a state in the first place.

'Thanks, Breeny, you're a mate.'

'I know.' She gave a half-hearted smile. 'I think you

should ring Fran up this evening. I don't understand why she hasn't come to school today.' There was a pause, then after a moment she added, 'And I should keep clear of Phil for a while if I was you.'

My stomach somersaulted. It was no good, I had to know. 'I remember I said some awful things about Fran in the pub, but did I say something stupid on the way home? I can't remember anything after I passed out.'

'Oh, I thought you remembered it all.' She looked embarrassed. 'Well you just said some stuff about him being the love of your life, and about how you and he should...'

'OK, enough!'

I saw him later in the day outside the changing-rooms. I think he saw me too, but he turned his back immediately and started talking to one of his friends.

As soon as I got home, I shut myself in Mum's bed-room to ring Fran. Her mother answered the phone.

'Yes, Fran is in,' she said guardedly. 'Who is it calling?'

'It's Charlie Hudson. I'm a friend from school.'

There was a pause. 'I don't think "friend" is a very good description from what she's been telling me,' said her mother. 'I'm afraid she doesn't want to speak to you. And if you're the person who persuaded her to go out drinking, then I don't think I want to talk to you very much either.'

'Oh, but I just wanted to ask why she hadn't come to school—'

'Look, I'm really very busy. Perhaps some other time? Goodbye.' The line went dead.

Wed 22nd Jan.
Dear God, Squirrel said to talk to you, so here I am. What

*am I supposed to do? I am truly sorry about what has
happened and I really want to put things right with Fran.
But how can I say sorry if no one will listen?*

Otherwise things seemed to have settled down on the
whole. Sabrina was her normal friendly self; but after a
couple of days there was still no sign of Fran at school.
When Mr Larkin took the register on Thursday
morning, I grabbed the opportunity to ask him where
she was. He gave a rather vague reply, something along
the lines of, no, she wasn't sick, there was some sort of
personal crisis, other than that he couldn't say. I was sure
he was hiding something, but it was hopeless trying to
get anything out of teachers.

Phil was still totally ignoring me.

At the weekend I saw Becky and Kate for the first
time since the fatal Sunday. They were all agog to know
what had happened. I played it very cool, and gave the
impression that it had been a very uneventful evening.

'What about Phil?' asked Kate. 'Are you going out
with him now?'

'Nope,' I replied, in a don't-ask-any-more-questions
kind of voice. They could hardly fail to notice that
although Phil had made an appearance at SPs this week,
he was keeping as far away from me as possible.

Luke came over. 'Hi, Charlie, how are things? We
missed you last week. It was really good, wasn't it, girls?'

'Yeah, brilliant,' agreed Becky. 'The speaker was excellent. He brought his band with him, they were unreal!'

Luke was looking at me. 'Everything OK, Charlie?'

'Fine, everything's fine.'

'Fran's away again this week. You're the one who
brought her here – do you think she's stopped coming?'

'How should I know?' I snapped. 'I'm not her

minder!'

'All right, all right, I only asked,' said Luke mildly. 'Perhaps I'll get Debbie to give her a buzz during the week.'

I wondered whether Fran would tell Debbie all the things I had said. That would well and truly put a full-stop to my brilliant evangelist image.

Mon 27th Jan.
Still no sign of Fran at school. She's been off a whole week now. What have I done? I think I'm going to have to pluck up the courage to go and see her.

I rang Mum after school to let her know where I was, then caught the bus to the top of Fran's road. I knew where she lived although I'd never actually been there. She'd invited me loads of times, but I'd always made some excuse.

It was already dark, and there was nobody about in the road. I stood on her doorstep and pressed the bell. The resulting chime sounded as loud as Big Ben and echoed all down the street; it was all I could do not to turn tail and run away.

Fran's startled eyes peered round the curtain of her front room. A couple of minutes later her mother opened the door. She obviously knew who I was.

'Yes?'

My mouth went dry. 'Could I speak to Fran for a minute?'

'No, I don't think so. She doesn't want to see you.'

'Well, could I just… it's just that we all wondered why she was off school, and if I could do anything…?'

'No,' said Fran's mum, her lips all tight and straight, 'I don't think you can do anything. In fact if you want to know the truth, I'm trying to get her transferred to another school. She's never been happy at Tatbury High and all the things you said to her last week were just the final straw. She feels that nobody likes her, that she's stupid and ugly, and I can't get her to go back. There. Are you satisfied?'

Dumbfounded, I stuttered. 'But I never meant…'

'No, I'm sure you never meant. Look, it's not just you, it's everyone, she's just had enough of that place.'

I was totally at a loss for words. I muttered something about being terribly sorry and hoping she would change her mind, then said goodbye and left.

Tues 28th Jan.
I'm not a bully, really I'm not. I'm not like Pete Smith or one of those bitchy girls in Year 11. If only I'd had the guts to stand against the crowd, if only I'd never said all those things I didn't mean, if only I'd never had all that drink. If only I could put the clock back and start again.

Wed 29th Jan.
Freezing cold day. All the puddles are covered in ice. Everyone at school huddled round radiators whenever possible. Allowed to eat lunch in classroom instead of being thrown out into the cold, which only happens when temp goes below about -20.

Phil hasn't even looked in my direction. Have decided the only course of action left to me is to become a nun. A silent order would be best, so that I will have to keep my big mouth shut.

In the meantime am concentrating all my energies on history essay.

10

The first day of February was the worst day of my life.

The weather was even colder, there was ice on the inside of my bedroom window in the morning, and all the trees were covered in frost. All down the road people were having trouble starting their cars.

School was no better; in spite of serious revision, my mark in the French test was very low. As if this wasn't enough, I got involved in an argument with Denise Luckworth who said Christians didn't know how to enjoy themselves and were against people having fun. I actually found myself wishing Fran was there to take my side. To crown it all, on the way home I slipped over on a patch of ice, causing a huge bruise to swell up on my left shin.

I got in to find Josh alone in the house. Mum had just rung to say her bus had broken down, so she would be home on the later one.

I made a cup of tea and went upstairs to do some more work on my history essay. Josh followed me up, obviously at a loose end.

'Charlie, will you play Football Manager with me?'

'Not now, Josh, go away and watch telly or something, can't you?'

He made no effort to move but leaned against my desk picking up one thing after another, examining each item with great interest.

'Josh! Buzz off!'

Still no response. Instead he started singing in a tiny and unbelievably irritating little voice, 'Charlie fancies Phi-il, Charlie fancies Phi-il…'

I aimed a hefty swipe in his general direction. He dodged to avoid the blow and sent the little pot on the corner of my desk flying onto the floor, breaking it into several pieces and scattering earrings all over the carpet. It was the pot Squirrel had made for my Christmas present; not valuable, but the most precious thing on my desk.

Suddenly all the things that had gone wrong with my life came together in one blinding moment of wild anger. 'You stupid prat! Look what you've done!' I shrieked at him, leaping to my feet in a furious rage. Josh, clearly sensing that this was more than a normal outburst looked round nervously for an escape route.

'I don't care!' he shouted. 'You're just a stupid girl anyway!' He ran to the door. 'I'm going to Jamie's house! At least he'll do things with me!'

There was the sound of footsteps pattering down the stairs, a pause as he stopped to pick up his football from the hall cupboard, then a draught of icy air and a loud bang as the front door slammed shut.

Blessed peace in the house for a moment. Jamie's house was only a few yards down the street on the other side of the road, and the street lighting was good, so he would be all right.

I took some deep calming breaths and turned back to my history essay.

As I picked up my pen there was the most almighty squeal of car brakes outside in the road, followed by a loud bang and the sound of breaking glass. A brief silence followed, then running footsteps and voices shouting.

My heart seemed to stop beating.

I raced downstairs and into the street, as if in a dream.

A few yards up the road, almost opposite Jamie's house, was a blue car at right angles across the road. It had obviously skidded on the icy road and hit a lamp post, making a large dent in the bonnet and virtually destroying the lamp post. The cause of the skid became terrifyingly clear as I got nearer. In the dazzling beam of the crumpled car's headlights lay a small heap, and that small, very still heap was wearing Josh's school jumper. His face was a ghastly white, apart from a thin trickle of crimson blood which ran down his left cheek.

'Josh! Josh!' I screamed and started crying hysterically.

The driver of the blue car, who looked nearly as pale as Josh although he didn't seem to be hurt, stood staring at the scene of catastrophe in complete bewilderment.

'It wasn't my fault,' he kept saying, 'he just came out of nowhere... I couldn't stop... not my fault... not my fault...'

'Do you know him, dear?' asked a woman who I vaguely recognised from the newsagent's shop.

'He's my brother!' I managed to get out between sobs.

She laid her coat over him to keep him warm, and the man from the car behind called for an ambulance on his mobile phone. It arrived in a very short time, just as

Mum, laden with several bags of shopping, was getting off the bus outside our house. I could see her, putting down her load and fumbling for her front door key, then pausing and looking down the street to see what all the commotion was about. First an expression of surprise, then sympathy, then dawning horror as she saw me standing on the pavement surrounded by people.

'Charlie? Are you all right? Where's Josh?' and then as she saw the small shape in the road, 'Josh? *Where's Josh?*'

Squirrel took me back to her house while Mum went to the hospital in the ambulance with Josh. Dad went there too, straight from work, as soon as he heard.

He wasn't dead – that was all we knew. We would just have to wait for the doctor to tell us how bad it was. Mum promised to ring as soon as she had any news.

Squirrel tucked me up in bed in her spare room, but I knew I wouldn't be able to sleep. I kept thinking of the driver, standing in the headlights and staring in horror at what had happened.

It wasn't my fault, wasn't my fault, wasn't my fault.

I was awake most of the night. Eventually, near morning, I fell into a heavy sleep and was woken by the sound of the phone.

It was Mum calling from the hospital. Apparently Josh had a ruptured spleen, whatever that meant, and a broken leg. He also got a nasty bang on the head as he fell, which explained the blood on his forehead. The most serious bit was the spleen: Mum said he would need to have an immediate operation to remove it, as it was too difficult to repair with surgery.

She sounded really strange, not a bit like her usual self. After she had rung off, I shut myself in the bathroom with Squirrel's big encyclopaedia of family health and turned to the section under the letter 'S'.

Spleen, ruptured, I read. *Most often as the result of a car crash or a fall from a height. If there is severe bleeding, it may be fatal.* There was a lot more stuff about what a spleen is and why you need it and how you manage without one.

I sat on Squirrel's furry white bathroom rug and cried and cried.

Squirrel must have heard because she came and knocked gently on the door.

'Charlie? Are you all right? Can I come in?'

I washed my face with a cold wet flannel, then unlocked the door.

Squirrel peered round, her face all wrinkled up with worry. At the sight of her I started crying again, crying and crying as if I would never stop.

'Oh, Squirrel,' I sobbed into her shoulder, breathing in her familiar lily-of-the-valley soap smell, 'it's all my fault! If I'd never shouted at him, he would never have run out and the car would never have hit him. If I hadn't got myself in such a state over Phil and everything, I wouldn't have been so irritated with him. He was only being his usual Josh-ish self. And now he's going to die, and it's all my fault!' There was no hiding behind an image now, the real me was there for all the world to see.

'There, there,' said Squirrel rocking me against her shoulder like she used to do when I was little, even though I was taller than her now. 'He's not going to die. You'll see. It'll be all right.'

She led me downstairs to her old saggy sofa where she used to cuddle me when I was a toddler with a scraped knee, and we sat there together and prayed for Josh. Then I cried some more and Squirrel cried a bit too.

In the evening Dad rang, and I could tell from his voice that things were better.

'He's had the op,' said Dad. 'He hasn't come round properly from the anaesthetic yet, but it looks as though he's going to be OK, although we have to wait twenty-four hours to be sure. And then he'll have to have further observation for the bang on his head. And of course his leg's all in plaster. But I think it's all going to be all right.'

I couldn't speak. I'd started to cry again, this time with relief.

Early the next day Mum rang again to say Josh had come round from the anaesthetic and was now in the intensive care unit. She didn't know how long he would be there, as that depended on how quickly he started to recover.

'Can I come and see him?' was the first thing I asked.

'Yes, you can come for a short visit this evening. But it will have to be brief, he's still not at all well, and you must be prepared for the fact that he looks dreadful; all full of tubes and things.'

Dad appeared at lunchtime for a sandwich with me and Squirrel. He had come home to get Josh's pyjamas and other stuff he would need in hospital. I'd never seen him look so tired and strained.

'How's Helen bearing up?' asked Squirrel.

'Not too bad, although I think she's suffering a bit from shock. It must have been an awful moment, getting off that bus and realising it was Josh lying there.'

As the day went on other people started to ring and call. Josh had been the subject of prayers at church and everyone wanted to know how he was.

Becky and Kate dropped a note through Squirrel's letter box:

Dear Charlie,
We were so sorry to hear about Josh's accident.
All thinking of you and we'll say a prayer for you
at SPs tonight. Is there anything we can do?
Loads of love, Becky and Kate.

It was a really good feeling to know that people were thinking about us.

In the evening Squirrel went off to church, and Dad took me into the hospital. Hospitals always make me feel lost, and today was no different. As soon as we walked through the main entrance, everything seemed so busy and organised. There were lots of people bustling around in uniform, people carrying big bunches of flowers, people in dressing gowns and hundreds of signs pointing you in different directions to Outpatients and Wards and X-ray departments. As we stepped into the lift a nurse was coming out of it, pushing a very old woman in a wheelchair. The woman's head was sagging onto her chest and there was dribble coming out of the corner of her mouth; she looked as if she was dead already. I wondered how Josh, who hardly ever even had a cold, would cope with all this going on round him.

It seemed to be miles down the corridor to Intensive Care. Mum met us at the door, she had been sitting by Josh's bed all day. Although they had warned me he looked awful, I was quite unprepared to be quite so shocked by his appearance. He was lying on his back, looking incredibly small on the big hospital bed, and his face was white as a sheet, although, thank goodness, there was no sign of the blood that had been there after the accident. There was a tube going into his hand and another one disappearing under the blankets into his tummy. I had this strange feeling that he was someone

111

else, not the Josh I saw and fought with every day.

I went close to the bedside and his eyes opened.

'Hallo, Charlie,' he said very quietly, and smiled a little. His eyes closed again.

'He's very sleepy,' said Mum. 'They've given him all sorts of painkillers so he's quite doped up.'

For once in my life I couldn't think of anything to say to him, so I just sat by the bed and stroked his hand. I stayed like that for about fifteen minutes, till Mum said she thought I had been there long enough. Dad was going to stay with him overnight, and she would come back home with me.

When we got home she sank into a chair, completely shattered. I went to the fridge to see what I could find for us to eat. There was some leftover chicken casserole from Thursday evening, the night before the accident. I remembered the evening when we had it, all sitting round the table together. It seemed like another lifetime. I wondered whether it would be safe to reheat the casserole in the microwave, and decided to take the risk as there was nothing else. I needn't have bothered – neither of us was really hungry.

At eight o'clock I went to bed and fell asleep instantly.

I felt a bit better the next day, although I was still inclined to burst into tears at the slightest thing. I wasn't too enthused at the idea of going to school but as Mum pointed out, I would only sit and mope if I stayed at home, so I might as well go. That was when I discovered that having a major disaster in your life makes you into an instant overnight celebrity: everyone wanted to hear all the gory details. It was a huge relief when the last bell went and I could escape at the end of the day.

112

I went straight to the hospital, which was only a few minutes walk away from school. Long walk down the corridors, again following the signs for intensive care. I found the right door and peeped round.

Josh was gone.

Total panic. Had he died in the night and no one had told me?

A nurse walked briskly past me and I grabbed at her.

'My brother! Where is he? Where's he gone?'

'Who is your brother?' she asked, gently removing my clutching hand from her arm.

'Josh Hudson. Is he – is he…?'

'Oh, Josh, let me see, yes. He's been moved to Balmoral. No need to keep him here any longer, he's well on the mend.'

Indescribable relief. A few instructions as to how to find Balmoral and I was off down the corridor once more.

Balmoral ward was a large airy room with big windows and sun shining into every corner. I immediately spotted Josh in the corner bed, propped up on pillows and talking to Squirrel who had pulled a chair up close to his side. There was another boy, a bit older, in the bed next to him who was sitting up and joining in the conversation. Josh still looked very pale and he still had the tube running into his hand, but apart from that he looked a hundred times better than the day before.

Squirrel moved aside to make room for me and we chatted for a bit. I told him about all his schoolfriends asking after him and then helped him open some get-well cards. The boy in the next bed was called Andy, who was recovering from an operation on his knee.

After a while Josh began to look quite tired, so I got

up to go. As I was leaving I bent over him and whispered so that no one else could hear, 'I never meant it to happen. I'm so sorry, Josh. *So* sorry.'

He looked up with big brown eyes and gazed at me in amazement. 'What on earth for? It was just an accident. I don't know what you're on about.'

He really meant it, he didn't even remember me shouting at him.

'Tell you what, though, Charlie,' he said as an after-thought, as I picked up my school blazer. 'Could you bring in my collection of football stickers tomorrow? I want to do some swaps with Andy. He's a Man U supporter, can you believe it? *Yuk.*'

The nurse was right, he was definitely on the mend.

As he got better he began to have streams of visitors. Mum and Dad found it hard to get him to themselves. His class teacher went in with a pile of work for him to do, but even that didn't seem to dampen his spirits. He spent much of his time sitting on his bed playing cards on the locker with Andy. His broken leg was in plaster and was decorated with a selection of autographs, art-work and graffiti, in varying degrees of originality. Things like 'the break will do you good' and 'pull the other one, it hurts less' and 'have you heard Josh Hudson's excuse for missing school? He hasn't got a leg to stand on'. And a staggeringly imaginative contribu-tion from Andy in the next bed: 'Man United are Great'. Josh tried to scribble this one out with biro, but Andy had used a thick black felt-tip, so the shameful message was there to stay until the plaster came off.

Fri 7th Feb.
End of a very busy week. Have been to see Josh every day after school; every day he's looked more and more perky.

114

The nurses all flock round him and fight to be the lucky one to take his temperature. He hardly complains at all, even though he must be uncomfortable a lot of the time. I don't suppose he's ever had so much attention in his whole life before.

House is incredibly quiet without him.

Never thought I'd say this, but I really miss him.

11

Two days later I went to the hospital after school and, as I was going through the main entrance, almost walked straight into Fran coming out the other way.

'Charlie! I hoped I would find you here.'

'Fran! What are you doing here?'

'I popped in to see Josh. I only just heard what happened to him; because of not having been to school for a while, I'm always the last to hear everything. Poor you, Charlie, what an awful time you must all have had.' She looked round the entrance of the hospital. 'Is there somewhere we can go for a cup of tea or something? Have you got time?'

'Yes, of course, there's a Red Cross place through those doors.' I led her through to the little area where you could get a drink and a snack, and we bought ourselves some tea and biscuits.

'I've been trying to talk to you for ages,' I said, wondering if she was still furious with me. 'Your mum kept sending me away, so in the end I gave up, but I've been really worried about you, especially when you didn't turn up at school; and I desperately wanted to say sorry for all those terrible things.'

'It's OK, I know,' she said holding up a hand to stop the flow of words, 'and it's true, I did tell Mum not to answer the door or phone to you. I just didn't want to see anybody.'

'Are you still mad at me?' I asked, not sure if I wanted to hear the answer.

Fran stirred her tea. 'I was for quite a long time,' she said. 'The thing was, I'd looked up to all the people at St Matthew's so much, and I just couldn't believe that you could be so horrid. Just like Pete Smith and everyone else at school. It was such a let-down. I really had thought that Jesus was the answer to everything until I saw how little effect he seemed to have on your life.'

Squirm. 'And now?'

'Now I know that Jesus is the answer to everything.'

'But what changed your mind?'

'It was Debbie. She came round to see me. Do you remember that talk she gave on forgiveness before Christmas?' I did remember, it had been at the back of my mind ever since.

'Well, she reminded me again of what she had said about the church being made up of sinners, not people who are perfect, and that those are the people who most need God. And I realised that of course that included you. So who was I to go on feeling angry with you when we belong to the same family and both have so much to learn?'

Silence for a moment. I thought of Josh and how he and I both belonged to the same earthly family and how I needed to learn to live with him too. Much the same idea really. Both Josh and Fran seemed to be so much

117

better at loving than me.

I felt the words must be said, even though I seemed to be constantly apologising these days. 'Well, I am most terribly sorry—' but Fran interrupted. 'It's OK. Forget it. Have another biscuit.'

We munched together in a friendly way, then I said, 'Fran?'

'Mm?'

'I'm glad we're part of the same family.' It sounded a bit like a line from a dreadful Hollywood B movie, but I meant it anyway.

Fran beamed one of her most enthusiastic smiles that under any other circumstances would have sent me running for the door. 'I know. It's brilliant, isn't it? Now we're friends again, perhaps we could go out on Saturday together? With Sabrina, of course.'

A hundred excuses rushed through my brain. I shut them all out and gritted my teeth.

'Excellent idea. I'll give you a ring later in the week when we know what we're doing.'

Home Ec lesson. Sabrina and I were making cream of vegetable soup. We made a good team. I peeled the vegetables and she chopped them.

There was the usual high level of noise in the cookery room, so I took the opportunity to say, 'I saw Fran yesterday.'

'*Did* you? Where?'

'At the hospital. She'd come to visit Josh.' I concentrated on scraping a carrot. 'Actually, I think she really came to see me.'

'Wow.' Sabrina stopped chopping for a moment and stared at me. 'What did she say?'

'Well, I suppose you could say that basically we're

mates again. She wants to do something with you and me next Saturday. Go out somewhere or something.'

'Wow,' said Sabrina again.

Mrs White, the HE teacher, appeared by our table.

'Are you two ready to be liquidised? Come on, you pair of slowcoaches, you haven't even sweated yet. And Sabrina, how many times have I got to tell you not to wear nail varnish in the Home Economics Room?'

She went on to the next table, tutting under her breath as she went.

I must have looked a bit startled, as Sabrina said, 'It's the vegetables that have to sweat, not you, wally. It's a cookery term. Don't you ever listen in class? Anyway, go on, is Fran going to come back to school?'

'I don't know. She's thinking about it. Her mum's been trying to get her into Grange Road, but without much success so far, so maybe she will come back. Can't help feeling it slightly depends on how we treat her.' I didn't say it but I was thinking it really depended on how *I* treated her.

Sabrina digested this information, then said, 'So where shall we go on Saturday?'

We spent some time discussing plans for the weekend, until Mrs White advanced menacingly with the dreaded liquidiser. By then we had decided to go skating at the new rink in Fenchester, although I would have to borrow money from Dad as I was skint again.

Fri 14th Feb.
Valentine's Day. Surprise, surprise, nothing for me.

Becky got one, she thinks it's from a boy at her school who she rather likes, and Sabrina got three. She says she doesn't know who any of them are from. I wonder.

Cleared the garage out for Dad in the evening and

earned enough money for skating. Will try to save instead of spending all my money straight away in future. Well, I can always dream, can't I?

Josh has a slight infection so will have to stay in hospital longer than he had hoped. He is beginning to feel very bored, especially as Andy went home last Tuesday.

The new rink was excellent – brilliant music and loads of room for everyone. I fell over a few times but without causing permanent damage. Fran seemed to have a good time; she kept saying things like, 'Isn't this fun?' and, 'It's so nice to be here with you and Sabrina!' every time we passed each other. She spent most of the time on her bum, but didn't seem to mind at all. You had to admire the girl. In her place I'd have walked off the ice after the first fifty falls.

It was the beginning of half-term and the weather was beginning to warm up. One afternoon halfway through the week I went into the hospital to see Josh and found him sitting up in the chair by his bed, smiling from ear to ear.

'I can come home tomorrow!' were his first words. 'The doctor says the infection is all cleared up and he thinks I can manage on crutches. So you can come and take me away in the morning!'

Mum gave him such a big hug he had to beg for mercy.

'Oi, mind my scar!' he gasped. 'It's not healed yet. You'll all have to treat me with great care, you know. I'm in a very Delicate Condition.'

'So no football for a bit?' said Mum.

'Oh, I don't know about that. I had a go with Andy down the ward using my teddy as the ball. I can hit a really big whack with my crutch,' he said proudly. 'And there's nothing to stop me going to watch, even if I can't play.'

The unfamiliar silence in the house was about to disappear.

He could get around the house very efficiently on his crutches when he wanted something in a hurry. The rest of the time he lounged around on the sofa giving everyone orders, until I began to wonder how long it would be before we all went on strike. Several of his schoolfriends came round to inspect his operation scar on the day he got home. They were all deeply impressed.

After half-term Fran came back to school.

She came in late, after assembly. At Registration Mr Larkin told us she was coming back, and then said a few things about bullying and how we should treat each other with respect.

I noticed Pete Smith leaning back in his chair with his arms crossed and a smirk on his face, but when Fran came into the room he just gazed out of the window and whistled a little tune to himself. She slipped into her place and started unpacking her books as if she had never been away.

At breaktime she and I went to the tuckshop with Sabrina and bumped into Phil on the way. He hadn't said more than about ten words to me since that gruesome evening in the pub, and those were only to ask how Josh was; but when he saw Fran, he stopped.

'Hi, Fran. Great to see you back.'

'Hi, Phil,' she replied, nervously fiddling with the strap of her school bag.

He grinned and walked on without a glance in my direction. At least I hadn't ruined *her* relationship with him, even if I'd ruined my own.

Fran saw my long face and gave my arm a little pat. 'Cheer up, Charlie. I'm sure you'll be friends again soon. Anyway, there's loads of other gorgeous hunks out there.'

I smiled weakly.

I realised that Sabrina was listening to this little exchange with interest, but she made no comment.

It was Becky's birthday. I rang her up to wish her many happy returns and to ask what it was like to be fifteen.

'Much the same as fourteen,' she said, 'except I can go to all Those Films now.'

I didn't even feel particularly envious. Josh's accident seemed to have changed my whole view of what was really important in life.

Wed 5th March.
Life pretty well back to normal, although Josh will be on crutches for quite a long time yet.

Fran came to SPs on Sunday and seems to have decided to stay at Tatbury High for the time being. Pete Smith and mates still make the occasional half-hearted attempt to have a go at her, but she seems to be able to cope with it as long as Sabrina and I are there to support her.

'Are you all right, Charlie?'

It was a crisp, sunny Saturday afternoon and Luke and Debbie had organised one of their on–the–spur–of–the–moment outings for the youth group. Today it was a walk up Gorse Hill, a local beauty spot just outside the town. It was still very cold, but there was a feeling of spring in the air, and the higher we climbed the warmer the exercise made us. I had been walking by myself for a while, a little behind the others who were all racing each other to the top, and it was Debbie who had dropped back and was now walking beside me.

'I'm OK,' I said, in answer to her question, 'I was just thinking about things.'

'You've had a tough time lately, haven't you?' she said sympathetically. I remembered that she was the one who had picked up the pieces with Fran after the awful night at the pub. There was no point in trying to put on a holy front with her, she knew all about me.

'You must think I'm a total disaster area,' I said, kicking a stone up the path in front of me.

'No, I don't,' said Debbie, 'I think you're a very normal young lady. But I do sometimes wonder who is the real you. Sometimes I think you're one person, and then you say or do something that makes me think you're someone quite different.'

I looked at her sharply. How did she know? 'It's true,' I said, 'I am lots of different people. It feels as though each me is like a different outfit that I put on and take off to impress the person I'm with. Only, after Josh's accident it was as if all the clothes were taken away, and I'm frightened that the me I'm left with isn't very nice. I don't think I want anyone to see the me underneath.' I stopped on the path and looked back at the view to get my breath, and added, 'Does that sound totally bonkers?'

'Not at all bonkers,' said Debbie, 'and in fact it's not even a new idea. Paul in the Bible was always talking about putting things on and dressing up. Only in his case it was good things like a new self, and love. And armour.'

'*Armour?*' I had a sudden weird picture of myself turning up at school in chain mail, with a visor over my face.

'Yes, the armour of God. The belt of truth, the shield of faith, the sword of the Spirit – he meant the Bible by that – and lots of other things. He says if you wear these things then you are ready to fight any temptation that comes at you.'

'Does it really say that?' It was amazing to think of a first-century Christian thinking about what he was going to wear.

'Yep. And above all to put on "love which binds everything together in perfect harmony". Think about it. Those old clothes of yours are all homemade, outfits you've invented for yourself in the hope that they'll impress everybody. But if you're dressed in the sort of things that God provides for you, you'll be wearing a designer label. After all, he designed *you*, didn't he? So isn't he bound to know best exactly what you need to put on?'

I thought back to what Squirrel said ages ago about it being what was inside you that was important, not how you appeared to others. It all began to make sense.

'I suppose love is the crucial thing,' I said slowly. 'I've been so busy trying to make everyone love me that I've forgotten about showing love to them. I should think God's just about given up on me.'

'Never,' said Debbie, grinning broadly. 'God will never give up on you. Even when you let go of him, he's still holding on to you. Race you to the top?'

'No chance. It's bad enough being made to walk up hills without having to run up them.'

Fri 7th March.
Daffodils in front garden coming out.
Phil actually spoke to me outside school this afternoon. Well, it was more of a nod and a smile, not really much in the way of words, but it's a start. Things are looking up.
Don't know how he feels about God and stuff, he only seems to turn up to SPs when he feels like it, and often argues with what people say there. One of his mates at

124

school told me that he'd signed up for the Tatbury Rugby Club, so perhaps his mum's decided it'd be a good thing after all. At least it means he'll have less time for Spike and co. Hope God's holding on to him too.

Sabrina could say very unexpected things sometimes. We were testing each other on French irregular verbs one dinnertime, when quite out of the blue she said, 'I'd really like to go to church with you on Sunday. You know, your youth group and everything. Would I be allowed?'

I was totally gobsmacked. 'Well, yes. Of course you would. But why the sudden change of mind? I thought you had all Christians labelled as sad deluded misfits who didn't know how to have a good time?'

She looked slightly sheepish. 'Well, actually it was Fran who convinced me it might be worth giving it a try.'

'*Fran?*' I tried to grapple with the concept of Fran as a mass evangelist. It was too bizarre to contemplate.

'The thing is, it really seems to work for her. I mean let's face it, Charlie, you were pretty vile to her. But she really seems to have forgiven you. And she seems so different these days, more, more... well you know.'

It was true. She was still the same old eager, irritating, prattling twit, but somehow there was a new confidence about her. As if whatever people said to her, she knew deep down that there was someone who really loved her. It was weird, but for some strange reason it made you want to love her too.

I nodded. 'I know what you mean. Well, of course you can come, it'd be great. But you do realise what you're in for? Singing and prayers and stuff?'

'Yeah, yeah, I'm not stupid.'

I wondered whether to tell her not to wear anything

too outrageous, then decided against it. Sabrina was Sabrina, they would have to accept her as she was.

I needn't have worried, she really enjoyed herself. She came in time for the evening service, and stayed for SPs. Luke and Debbie were running a question and answer session and Sabrina seemed to be really intrigued. She asked all sorts of questions herself and joined in the discussion as if she'd been coming for years. Kate and Becky were delighted to see her, and needless to say, Fran was thrilled.

In a quiet moment afterwards I asked her what she had thought of it.

'Very interesting. And that Luke – he's something else!'

'Steady, girl, he's married!'

'Only kidding. No, it was good. I'll come again.'

Nothing surprised me any more.

Good Friday, 27th March.

Becky rang, full of the news that Luke and Debbie are expecting a baby. We'll all be queuing up to babysit.

Went to Good Friday service with Sabrina. Becky's dad talked about the cross and what it meant. Nothing we do is so bad that we can't be forgiven. Sabrina very quiet and thoughtful. Felt pretty thoughtful myself.

Easter Day, 29th March.

Woke up to brilliant sunshine.

Easter bunny came as usual and hid chocolate eggs all round the garden. Have pointed out to parents that am now far too old for this sort of thing, but fortunately no one takes any notice. Breakfast, then off to church.

Fantastic service. Church packed, awesome music; strings, guitars, drums and trumpet, singing loud enough *to be heard for miles around. Fortunately, no bagpipes.*

Everyone was there. Becky with all her brothers and sisters, Kate with her sister and both her parents. (They had no reservations about going to church on Easter day, as major Christian festivals are to be encouraged as a part of British culture.) Phil with his mum and older brother, Fran and Sabrina. And Sabrina had brought her dad.

I spotted Squirrel standing next to the wall by a new banner which was embroidered with hundreds of daffodils dancing in the wind. Underneath in big gold letters were the words: 'Life in all its fullness'. Squirrel was wearing what appeared to be a bird's nest on her head, but under closer inspection it turned out to be a new hat.

We sang a hymn, and then Becky's dad came to the front of the altar steps. He faced the congregation and raising both his hands, declared joyfully in a loud, deep voice, 'Christ is risen!'

I thought about the resurrection and the amazing new life that burst out that first Easter day. That's real life, the sort of life you discover when you stay close to God and live the way he wants you to, rather than trying to please everyone else. The sort of life that Squirrel lives. Life in all its fullness.

The thing is, I knew that *now*, but would I remember it when the heat was on?

I turned round and caught Squirrel's eye across the church. She was smiling broadly at me.

I smiled back and turned to the front again to join in the response.

'He is risen indeed. Alleluia!'

Other books from Scripture Union

In the Spotlight
Eleanor Davies

Dan and Jess first meet when they
are cast as an Ugly Sister and the
Fairy Godmother in a school panto.
Their friendship develops offstage
but it's not plain sailing and each has
different expectations.

ISBN 1 85999 440 7
Price £3.99

Zero in: The essential teen survival guide
Liz and Anna Hinds

Covering both Christian
and general contemporary
issues, this is a practical
look at everyday life, fully
indexed and packed with
humour but with a serious
edge. From Alcohol to Zits – it's the A–Z you've been
waiting for.

ISBN 1 85999 190 4
Price £3.50

**Available from your local Christian bookshop or from
Scripture Union Mail Order, PO Box 5148,
Milton Keynes, MLO MK2 2YX
Tel: 01908 856006 Fax: 01908 856020
Our usual post and packing rates for mail order apply**